Sour

Also by Iris Kain

Eternal Spring

Shadow Hunter

Sour

Iris Kain

To DJ and Ember, my real-life versions of Jake and Lorina.
Keep rocking, you two.

Chapter 1

Being a chaos witch sucks.

I was reminded of this as I stood behind the counter of Witch's Brew, my combination coffeehouse and metaphysical supply shop. The products are metaphysical. The coffee is, well, coffee. The front room had over a dozen four-person tables scattered around its space. The other two rooms had crystals, candles, herbs, books, wands. If it's witchy, I sell it. No one shopped at the moment, though.

Teens on their school lunch break stood frozen over their espressos and Ethiopian brews, staring at the man who had come into the door holding a gun. One held her cup of white chocolate latte inches from her perfectly lipsticked mouth, frozen as if by not moving, she would reduce her chances of being a target. Another's eyes darted around, searching for an opening to escape, but he didn't move, much like the skeletons I had posed in humorous ways around the store as Halloween decorations. I recognized him as a running back for the Gryphon High School football team. It contrasted starkly with the confident way he moved on Friday nights, running the football down the field.

The man with the gun, however, moved just fine. He strolled in with his shoulders back, the slightest twitch of a smile at the corner of his mouth, an automatic pistol of some sort gripped in his hand. Once upon a time, I might have been able to tell you what type. When my mother died, I went a little crazy learning about weapons. Despite the chaos that followed me seemingly every time I left my shop, none of it had involved weapons until now.

I'd lived a few lifetimes since then. That I can say that at twenty-six is a little sad, I guess.

I met the interloper's eyes with a steady gaze. I supposed being held at gunpoint would terrify most people, and while I didn't want to die, you don't go through as many shitty catastrophes as I do and not come out the other side a little more fearless. The gun man stared back, not intensely, but with intent.

Several of the kids took advantage of our locked eyes to sprint for the side door; others darted out the front and down the veranda stairs. I heard a cup fall with a crash to the floor and shatter. No biggie, I told myself. All the cups and plates were as mismatched as the salvaged furniture I used. Chair legs clattered, then the whole seat tipped to the floor with a *bang*.

Gun man's focus never wavered. His eyes were sea-foam green, his face bordering on gaunt with a fringe of light red beard. He made no move to aim, other than the vague ninety-degree angle he held at his elbow, and the short barrel pointed imprecisely in my direction. Several glass jars full of coffees, teas, and herbs stood on whitewashed shelves behind me, and I tried not to cringe at the thought of the shrapnel they might cause if hit by a bullet intended for me. At this close range, he'd have to be a shitty shot to miss.

Four kids remained. Regulars. I knew them all by name and had half of their mothers' phone numbers saved on my cell phone. They all looked terrified, and it touched me when I realized their concern was for my safety, not their own. Eight eyes darted back and forth between him and me, but their heads remained still.

Desperate to keep his attention on me, I spoke.

"What do you want?"

The gun man came to the counter. His imprecise aim tightened until the muzzle pointed more directly at my chest. My heart rate increased. My throat constricted. The heat from the unseasonably warm October air hit me, and it occurred to me that only seconds had passed since the front door closed.

"Your money," he snarled.

My mouth flattened, and I pushed a few buttons on the cash register screen, never breaking eye contact. I didn't want his eyes to leave mine—there were too many potential targets nearby. The drawer slid open, coins jingling and jostling as it hit the fullest extent. I grabbed a black plastic shopping bag with *Witch's Brew* written on the front in purple from under the counter and began filling it with my meager daily take, my mind racing.

I am protected by your might, oh mighty goddess, on this night.

Who robs a tiny shop like this knowing that its main clientele are high schoolers and a handful of southern pagans and novelty shoppers?

Protect those present from harm and fear, and keep your mighty presence near.

Past the shiny, short barrel, the man on the other side of the counter wore a clean polo and slacks that would be at home in any office for casual Friday. Middle-class. From this close, the smell of his aftershave and the oil from his gun wafted. He didn't look strung out on drugs or desperate, like the type who needed money.

If he doesn't need the money, then what—?

Mighty Athena, help me see. I trust your aid. So mote it be.

And she did. A veil lifted, and for the first time, I saw the containers of belladonna and vervain. The candles. The skulls, gourds, dried leaves, and bottles of mead I used as Samhain decorations. The hand-made brooms standing in the corner.

He wasn't here for my money. He was here because I was a witch.

Well, that's a dumb idea.

I put the last of the bills in the bag and handed it across the counter to him, but not before I made an almost imperceptible back-and-forth with my arm—a move so slight he had undoubtedly written it off as hand shaking in fear.

Fear inside my shop. The safest place on earth for me.

He gave me a smug smile and accepted the bag of bills, turned, and promptly tripped over a shard of ceramic from the shattered mug.

His ankle twisted with an audible *snap*. The load-bearing leg gave way under him, and he fell face-first onto the polished wood floor. The painted white moon in the center of the wooden floor became splattered with red from his newly broken nose. The pistol slipped from his grip and spiraled across the floor toward one of my regulars, a slender young woman named Cadence, who picked it up gingerly and handed it to her boyfriend, Jake. I wasn't sure if he knew how to fire a gun, but I knew he was a black belt, which was some comfort.

The tinkle of bells from the front of my shop drew my attention back to the entrance, where two police officers came in from the unseasonal heat, hands at their holsters. One student who fled must have called 9-1-1. Jake, still holding the gun, placed it on the table behind him, away from the robber, and put his hands up. I guess he thought they might assume he was the criminal with his long hair, death metal shirt, steel-toed boots, and black jeans and didn't want to give the cops any reason to suspect him.

"Murph? You OK?"

Officers Brandon Stout and Kenny Hendricks were regulars—two of the few people in Gryphon who didn't give a flip that I ran a shop full of witchy goods. The trail of chaos I often left in my wake meant police weren't an uncommon presence in my life, and over the years, both Stout and Hendricks had become friends of mine.

Stout, both his name and description, shot Jake a hasty glance, and his attention turned to the bloody would-be robber on the floor. Kenny—younger, fitter, and darker than his partner—switched his attention from me to the robber sprawled on my floor and back to me, waiting for an explanation.

"I… he…" my hands tried to say what my mouth couldn't, motioning back and forth from the robber to the cash register to the plastic bag of cash.

Another one of my regulars broke in. "He tried to rob her," Betony said, her purple hair shining in the light from the window. Her bright hazel eyes pleaded with them to listen. "He slipped and…" her hands performed the *voilà* motion toward the man on the floor. "See? The bag of money is right there." She pointed.

"His gun," Cadence added, pointing to where it lay on the table. "Jake took it away," she added. I was glad she clarified. It would explain any fingerprints that might get Jake in trouble.

Kenny's expression said it all as he shook his head. "Murphy." He wasn't smiling, but he wasn't stern, either. I sensed there might be voodoo or hoodoo in his family's past, but I wouldn't be the one to bring it up. The little hamlet of Gryphon lay in the Bible Belt of northern Alabama, after all. Most folks tend not to talk about things like that.

"I know, Kenny," I said, noting as I ran my hands through my hair that my purple nail polish almost matched Betony's hair. "Murphy's Law strikes again." I wiped my sweaty hands on my jeans and plopped into a wooden Queen Anne chair with a worn cushion. I tapped my Doc Martens on the floor, trying to let out some of my nervous energy.

Stout's kind, brown eyes met mine. He sighed and went to work. I sat, my heart still racing. Cadence, sweet young woman that she was, took a position at the door in case anyone came by to explain that it might be a few minutes before they could shop.

I tucked a strand of thick brown (chestnut, my best friend Hanna called it) hair behind my ear and leaned forward, resting my chin on my hands, my elbows on my knees.

Stout and Hendricks helped the struggling man to his feet. I noticed he had knocked out his two front teeth in his fall as well as cutting his cheek on another shard of the ceramic cup. As Stout snapped a pair of cuffs on his wrist, Hendricks got out a notepad to take down the details of the incident. Stout cuffed the man in front so he could use a paper napkin to stanch his bleeding nose, which would (based on the extremity of the damage) never look the same. Neither would his cheek. That gash needed stitches.

"Keep the change, asshole," I whispered. Cliché, but I couldn't stop myself.

☾○☾

Some people are green witches who have anything they touch blooming under their fingertips, use herbs to heal the deadliest of illnesses, befriend the worst-tempered animals, and help the most infertile person create life. Others are orange—astral witches who foresee the future in the stars, their tools, or inside still waters. My mother, Nora Blackwell, was brown—a kitchen witch—and could turn anything into the most delicious food you've ever tasted, could turn sugars and oils and vinegars and salts into potions and spells. Red witches create both love and glamour and sometimes use glamour spells to induce love. Everyone knows about black witches and their famous ability to curse and hex, but most people have never heard about the strength and power they often provide to grieving people and people in desperate need. Haunted house? Call a white witch to purge it. White witches also perform weddings and blessings on new babies. There are more common types, but those are the most often found in the United States.

Me? I'm a freaking chaos witch. Gray. Drab. Neither black nor white; the color of thunderclouds and boulders and mist. Well, my hair is chestnut brown, and so are my eyes, but whatever makes the rest of me is gray. I cause mayhem and destroy everything I am near.

Relationships? I learned not to bother trying to find my significant other when I hit sixteen. I was the one who broke hearts, fell for the best friend, or became bored after two dates. Sometimes one. One guy left in the middle of our first meal.

Work? Mother God, don't get me started. It's hard to get a career off the ground when every place you work closes, loses funding, or has everyone quit, get injured, or become ill within weeks of you starting.

Friends? Well, there I lucked out. I have Conall Barry, who has been my wingman since kindergarten—long before I discovered my power. And then there is Hanna Chava, my sister from another mister. Beautiful, composed, tall, tanned, stunning, and did I mention warded by her own mother's power? Yeah. She's impossible to kill—even her last name means "life" in Hebrew. That's the only thing keeping me from destroying everything we touch together. All of our mothers were in the same coven. They also died the same night. After that, there was no separating us.

I often wondered why Conall and Hanna never tried dating. The three of us had crested the mid-twenties, but none of us had stayed with anyone for long. My reason was obvious, but Hanna's list of suitors changed constantly. Her tiger's eye hair, smooth skin, and wide brown eyes drew men in like hummingbirds to honeysuckle. Add to that the mystery of being friends with a known town witch, and her allure was irresistible. Despite his dark hair, fit build, and super-friendly nature, introverted Conall led a homebody life. He seemed content to hang out at the store most evenings, even when he didn't have a client to read cards for, which was fine by me. Sometimes, being the only metaphysical store owner for miles made for interesting interactions, especially from local church folks. It was reassuring to have a backup with muscle.

I can't imagine what my mother's pregnancy might have been like, especially since she never intended to become pregnant. My conception wasn't planned. My mother didn't make it a secret that although my father held a special place in her heart, he'd never be a constant in her life. One of my great-great-grandmothers, who tried to warn the family of a coming gray witch, foresaw my birth.

I was prophesied.

I didn't know I was a chaos witch for almost half my life. I am the last of my family's line, and until things started going wonky around me, I'd never heard of a chaos witch. I guess we're rare. I've since learned we come around maybe once every three hundred years.

You don't get to pick what variety witch you are, and most witches exhibit a gift early. It's strange not to figure yourself before you reach the mid-teen years, but me... I caused chaos trying to decipher my witchiness.

I tried to be every other type, but nothing took off. Every plant I tried to raise in my high priestess LaDonna's thriving garden died. Every wildly inaccurate card reading I did outside of my home's warding caused more problems than it solved. Weather? Forget it—Mother Nature and I don't speak the same language unless it's about a coming storm. Relationships? Hell, how'm I supposed to help someone figure out what's going on with their love life when I hadn't experienced love? I had a gift for hexes (of course I did), but I never bestowed the strength in them that an average black witch does. I didn't have the heart.

The only trend I noticed was the path of destruction I wielded as I coursed through life. My elementary school? Burned to the ground when I was in 1st grade. A tornado ripped the roof off my middle school while I attended there. High school? Well, I dropped out of public school my sophomore year; I think the hormones combined with my witchy powers were too much for the Universe to handle. I went through a slew of teachers who got pregnant, moved, changed school districts—one died in a car accident. I spent a week in my bedroom racked with guilt after that last one. Every friend I made moved, was injured, or hated me within six months of meeting me. One poor soul broke her ankle *in my car* as I drove her to the airport to meet a flight. Her last words? "Murphy Blackwell, you are the *worst friend ever!*"

Yep. Chaos witch.

It freaking sucks.

Chapter 2

My hands still shook half an hour after Stout and Hendricks left. I longed for coffee to knock out the headache I'd been nursing since my power had caused the mugger to keel over and break his face on my floor. Cadence had kindly cleaned up the blood when she saw my reluctance to touch an object so intimately related to the intruder. There's a hell of a lot of power in a person's blood, and I'd already caused him enough damage. Yeah, he'd stolen from me, but my luck, I'd kill him by accident or something equally, freakishly bad.

"Mama Murph? You OK?" Bet crept closer and peered up to my face. Short and curvy, with long, wavy hair, Betony was the most outspoken of the troop of high school eccentrics who frequented my shop daily. At sixteen, she was too old to be my daughter, but she and her crowd had all started jokingly calling me "Mama Murph" when I began mothering them as if they were my kids. I made sure they did their homework, scolded them for skiving off classes or vaping. Betony might be like a second-mother-in-command, but she was the most mischievous one, and I adored her.

"I'll be OK," I assured her.

At six-foot-three, Jake loomed over everyone, and concern painted his freckled face. His wideset, downturned blue eyes reflected everything his mind turned over. Jake was a worrier. Tall, sturdy, dressed every inch in black, one would assume he left his house intending to kick someone's ass. Unbeknownst to them, Jake was a softy. A band nerd with the heart of a musician and the soul of a poet.

It wasn't like him to be so quiet, though, and I lost grip on my self-pity in concern.

"You OK, Jake?" I asked.

He frowned. "I don't like guns," he said. "They freak me out."

"Well yeah, they can kill people," Cadence chided, then shyly pulled her voluminous curls over her heart-shaped face with a long-fingered hand.

I scooted to the edge of my chair and stood on shaky legs. "Well, they didn't today."

"Did you hex him?" Bet asked. All the kids in the tight-knit clan knew about my witchery. They were among a handful of folks in town who understood that I am what most people only supposed or thought was a sales gimmick.

I scoffed. "Yeah, but it turned out a little stronger than I meant it to."

I pointed a finger at my chest and added, "Chaos witch, remember?"

"Isn't your store... you know... what's the word?"

"Warded?" I asked. "The first time by my mother, before I was born, when the town called this house Blackwell Manor. She was a lot stronger than I am. Her coven and I have kept the wards up steadily since then."

"I thought your mother was a kitchen witch," Jake asked.

"She was. You should see the kitchen in this place." I jerked a thumb toward the swinging doors that led to a chef's kitchen in the back. "It wasn't me who put it there. But to answer your question, any witch can protect themselves, their families, and their homes—they don't have to be any specific type."

"You don't cook," Cadence observed.

I laughed despite myself—a quick snort that caught me off guard. "No, but I *can* brew a helluva cup of coffee."

It was true. Hanna made all the pastries the coffeehouse offered in her kitchen. She was a kitchen witch like my mother, as well as a red witch who blended powerful love spells in her cooking cauldron. Though I hardly used the massive kitchen, it was one of my favorite rooms to spend time in my house. It was as if my mother's spirit permeated the fibers of the walls, the dark wood cupboards, the old combination oven and stove, and the herbs on the windowsill imbuing every facet with safety and warmth. The herbs survived thanks to some of my mother's old coven friends who checked on me on occasion and Hanna, witch extraordinaire.

Hanna was a rarity as well. Witches who harbored two gifts were almost as rare as chaos witches. Our friend Conall was an orange witch—blessed with the gift of prophecy like my grandmother. He could read tarot and use a pendulum to see the future.

One of my great-ancestors, Aislinn, an orange witch like Conall, predicted that I would be born and offered a foreshadowing of what my future would bring. Her poem sounded more like a spell than a prophecy, and I sometimes wondered if I wasn't foretold so much as cursed. This well-respected maternal ancestor wrote the words on a page of parchment handed down as a warning for five generations.

Farewell to care, farewell to order
Farewell to friends who seek safe quarter,

Unto our family comes a gray
And all our peace shall dash away.
Protect you well all you have wrought
Or all your efforts come to naught.
My family, please mind my behest
Or life will know naught but unrest.

My mother was aware of the prediction, but like great-great-grand-mother Dubheasa, (a red witch), great-grandmother Finola, (a white witch), and grandmother Siobhán (a rose witch), she chose to be a mother despite the prophesy. The coven told me over the years that I was loved and wanted, if not expected. (My mother referred to me as her "surprise.") Although my mother had nothing against the idea of terminating a pregnancy, it wasn't a choice she wanted for herself.

The coven told me a lot about my mother, as well as the great-great-great-great-grandmother who saw my coming birth. I sometimes won-der if that distant relative saw more than the havoc I would wield in the path of my life. Guess who is the one person on earth whose future my friend Conall can't predict? Did you guess me? Ding ding ding!

There is only one thing worse than knowing you're a chaos witch: not knowing what chaos you will cause. There's no way to prevent it.

Chapter 3

The handful of folks who came by in the evenings after the high school crowd scattered weren't there for the coffee. Most folks wandered in under the premise of buying a drink or a pastry that Hanna had made in her kitchen. They lingered near the shelves, idly eyeing the displays of candles and oils. They often paused to read the sign posted next to the curtain that covered the walk-in closet Conall had transformed into a private space to do his predictive readings three nights a week. They'd leave with a rock, a necklace, a candle—an object benign to the untrained eye—or with a whimsical gift from the singular store within 50 miles that stocked items for metaphysical needs.

Many women came by for Conall's readings, but I suspected that some returned for more than a glance at their future—more for a glimpse at Conall. Tall, dark-haired, with heavy-lidded eyes and a fit physique, Conall was a chick magnet, but one of the many qualities I loved about him was his obliviousness to his charm and good looks. He didn't date much, but not from lack of opportunity.

Sometimes, rarely, but sometimes, someone would wander in and ask for an athame, altar cloth, or a particular oil. I recognized a fellow witch when they called items by name. To a layperson, an athame was a dagger, dirk, or short sword. To a non-practitioner, an altar cloth was a blanket or a tapestry–sometimes a table cover. I always tried to help a fellow practitioner, but I had to bite my tongue occasionally. Nobody asks for belladonna with a noble motive. There's a reason I don't keep it on my shelves where people can see it. A person has to have a purpose to ask for that ingredient. It's not called deadly nightshade for nothing.

Even in Alabama, there is a need for the town witch. Folks might say they don't believe, but they do. If they didn't believe, why were so few able to meet my gaze?

Maybe it was the chaos that followed in my wake, but my guess is the word "witch" still held sway in these parts. People clung to fear for the cunning folk, and Gryphon wasn't a metropolis. In the past few years, what had once been a thriving town had shrunk to a small village, thanks to a supercenter opening in a town less than 15 miles away and two of Gryphon's major factories moving their production overseas.

The small group of friends who made my shop a second home would find their way to their favorite table soon after school let out. They'd buy a coffee, often one or two at a time, and always the drip coffee, never the more expensive cappuccinos or espressos. They'd talk about school and friends at first, chatting with a profusion of energy pent-up from having to sit at desks all day in school. As the evening wore on, they'd run more on coffee than anything, and the deeper conversations would come out.

Sometimes, Jake would bring in his guitar on Fridays after school, and I'd let him play a little. His playlist included several of my favorites—Nirvana, AC/DC, Metallica. He'd do "unplugged" versions of the tunes to keep it low, but every once in a while, I'd let him crank it up if business was slow and the customers were into it. Jake provided the guitar, Lorina with her curly hair parted in the middle, one side black the other fire engine red, provided the drums and captivating vocals that would have made sirens jealous.

I knew more about their lives than their parents ever would. I knew who had tried what drugs, who drank, who had already lost their virginity. I knew about their sexual orientation (or, in Betony's case, their lack of one).

I also knew my practice fascinated every one of them.

Outside my small combination house/shop realm, I was prone to bedlam. Inside my small, protected domain, I harnessed the craft I was born with safely, and most of the time, with frightening accuracy.

It wasn't what happened inside my haven that frightened me, but what people did with what I provided them sometimes which caused more problems than it solved. I performed protection and cleansing spells over everything that came into the shop and said a silent blessing over every item that left it. However, anyone who used products bought in my shop to perform a harmful spell had a head start before they cast a circle or lit their first candle.

My brow furrowed as a thought crossed my mind.

"What's the matter, Murph?" Cadence asked.

"That guy," I pointed at the door where the police had escorted the would-be robber out, "He shouldn't have been able to come in here."

"Why not?" Jake asked.

"It's *warded*," Betony explained animatedly, yet with a friendly smile. "By her mom and by her coven. We just covered this."

"Yeah," I agreed. I picked up a silver protection amulet and set it back down. "He shouldn't have been able to cross the threshold." Gently, I ran my fingers over the sigil on the amulet. "Theoretically, it shouldn't have even crossed his mind once he crossed the property line."

"How do you think he managed to come in?" Lorina asked as she leaned forward and put her slender elbows on the table. Her two-toned hair spilled over her forearms and nearly brushed the plate of pumpkin bread in front of her.

I shook my head. "The only thing I can think of is that maybe he had spells of his own."

"Stronger than your coven's?" Bet's eyebrows rose.

Although I considered myself a solitary practitioner most of the time, I was technically a member of the Lughaidh coven, the family of witches from which my mother descended, and the clan to which Hanna and Conall belonged. When I needed advice or occasional witchy help, they always came through. They extended invitations to join them at their meetings or for holidays. I often spent Yule or Mabon with them—it would be rude not to, and besides, they were the closest thing to family I had. The high priestess, LaDonna, came by often during full moons to help me renew the protection on my home, and every member of the coven used my shop to buy the ritual items they needed. They often stopped for tea and checked in with me, chatting for as long as they needed to ensure that my energy was positive and the home and shop were doing well.

My mother had been an exceptional practitioner, but some of these women—like LaDonna—wielded breathtaking power. I usually sensed them before they stepped out of their cars, and when they walked into my shop, I could see the waves of energy emitting like heat.

That someone—or a group of someones—may have power more potent than that wielded by the combined forces of the Lughaidh coven alarmed me. I covered my expression the best I could and pressed a smile onto my face.

"I'll talk to LaDonna," I assured them. "She'll know what to do."

"Maybe you should read your cards," Cadence suggested.

They loved watching me lay out a tarot spread, an art where I excelled within my shop—better than Conall, who had an excellent side hustle after his daily construction job from the closet-sized room off the coffee house where he did his readings. To his credit, Conall did better with pendulums and runes and pretty much any other method he used to divine the future.

The idea both drew and frightened me. I didn't read my spread often. I hated knowing what was coming. But if elements were working against me, I needed to prepare myself.

I nodded and headed back to the cupboard of personal items I kept inside the shop: a weathered, wooden green corner cabinet with brass rings held in place by gargoyle heads. The smell of my craft tools hit me as I pulled it open—fragrances of magnolia, ylang-ylang, myrrh, and cedarwood, of dried herbs, graveyard dirt, and beeswax candles.

I found the white silk tarot bag in the front right corner, where I always stored it. I took a bottle of purification spray and the cards back into the shop. Grasping the spray in one hand, I turned inward to the place where my power resided as I misted one of the tables out in the mostly deserted coffee shop. Betony came behind me with a towel and dried the surface reverently.

"...*Neither hope nor fear may gather here, but make the gods' intentions clear* ..."

I withdrew a black satin cloth from inside the bag that held my tarot and covered the table, muttering an incantation as I did.

"With this cloth, protection I place, to guard this table as a sacred space. May the work I do here stay with me. And as I will, so mote it be."

I started with a traditional Celtic Cross spread—the first two cards crossed in the center. Card three I placed below at a southerly position, and then four, five, and six at points west, north, and east. I added cards seven through ten to the right of this cross, starting at a southeast position, diagonal from cards three and six, and straight upwards for eight through ten.

"What's it mean, Murph?" Lorina asked. She'd been trailing my steps, watching from over my shoulder at a respectful distance, allowing me to focus my intention on the deck as I pulled the cards.

"A lot of not good, right?" Bet asked. I loved her, but her certainty was ill-placed. The cards were just that: cards. Most of what gave each symbol meaning was interpreted by the reader—in this case, me. Betony's belief that she had the power to read my spread showed a lack of maturity in her understanding of the craft. No witch should presume to understand the meaning behind what another witch has wielded. Few had that accord. Hanna and I came close. Conall and I also did exceptionally well.

My mother and I had made it an art.

I shrugged in response to Betony's reaction. While the meaning of some cards came to me quickly, others struck me as odd—which was abnormal. The cards never withheld secrets from me. "Yes, some of it.

The first card in the center bottom suggests me." The nine of swords card showed life in the present—an insecure, hooded figure gnawing on its hand. Indicative of worry, anxiety. Well, yeah.

"Stressed," Betony interjected.

I nodded. "Yes. The second could only be the gunman." The Fool seemed to be the symbol of my immediate challenge.

Card three: distant past. The High Priestess of the major arcana. Knowledge, a woman wise beyond her years. "Here," I pointed to the card, "is probably my mother." It described her perfectly. Even La-Donna, the high priestess, respected my mother's skills in the craft.

"Does that mean she has something to do with what is going on now?" Lorina asked, her voice a tentative balance between intrigue at ghost interfering and a touch of fear. She grabbed the ear of a wooden chair and pivoted it around so she could sit on it backwards with her arms along the top rail. Lorina had an uncanny knack for movements that would be masculine if anyone else did them. On her, they seemed suave and somehow charming.

"I can't imagine how, but I suppose it might be possible. And here," I pointed to the page of swords in the upright position, the page strolling down a lit path. Signaling someone perceptive, instinctive. "This shows an insightful person in my life."

"Who do you think that is?" Cadence asked. "Conall?" Whenever the kids think of someone who ostensibly *knew* things, their mind always went to Conall, and with good reason. The man had excellent prognostication skills.

Shaking my head, I had to admit I was clueless.

"You always know," Bet said. "That's not good."

This time she was right. For the cards to not reveal an answer, the universe had to be in a strange place. I placed my fingertips on the card and willed a face to come to mind. The card remained as empty as a switched-off television. "Nothing is coming to me."

"Could that mean you haven't met the person yet?" Jake asked.

"I hope so," I replied, hesitation apparent in my voice. "Anyway, this one," I pointed to the top card, "Shows my hopeful outcome." Ace of cups, upright. The artist had rendered it as a lovely woman clutching a jeweled cup to her chest. Abundance. Fullness. Beauty.

"That's, like, everyone's hopeful outcome," Lorina joked, but the sadness behind her eyes betrayed her. Lorina's family had all but discarded her, to hear her say it. The card must represent her hopeful outcome, too.

I moved on and pointed to card number six, showing my immediate future—an upright page of pentacles. A horned creature balanced a pentacle in one hand and peered at a book with another. An inventive, eager, creative pupil. "This is Bet," I said with a smile.

"How do you know?" Betony asked.

"Eager student," I replied with a shrug. "And you are, I'm guessing, a student in my immediate future. You're full of questions, but I don't mind. Here," I pointed to position seven, "Tells me what's making events happen in my life at the moment, what's affecting my circumstances."

"That's the Magician," Cadence remarked. Well, duh. I wasn't going to read into that one. Me.

The eighth position specified external influences, portents, warnings. Seven of swords—the universe was cautioning me about a deceptive person. Who would try to lie or deceive me? I shook my head and willed the fog clouding my vision to scatter, but it did nothing to clear my sight.

Ninth place, ten of cups, upright, showed hopes and fears. A wounded soldier hugged as he returned home. Family devotion. Love. Why would a card with positive implications be my hopes and fears? It was all so confusing.

The final one would show the product of the reading as a whole. The Wheel of Fortune, inverted. Did that mean what was coming was unexpected? Or unfortunate? Or both?

Well, shit.

Chapter 4

Since it was Friday, the shop closed an hour later than usual. And, as usual, my little band of adopted teens stayed to watch as Jake played his set. Tonight's list was more melancholy than usual, closer to Clapton unplugged, and I wondered if the events of the early afternoon had affected his music choices. Lorina seemed frustrated with his mellow music choices, which furthered my suspicion that things weren't well at home. Lorina was the yin to Jake's yang. Where Jake was reserved, Lorina was raucous. Where Jake was inexperienced, Lorina was worldly. Jake appeared sturdy, large-statured, indestructible, Lorina whip-thin. However, put the two of them together, and they made incredible music.

I wiped the last table with blackberry and clove spray at nine o'clock and locked the evening's funds into my small safe. Jake finished packing his rig, and Lorina helped him to load up in the Mitsubishi sports car parked outside. The strength in her slender body always amazed me. Betony and Cadence hung around and showed each other amusing things they found on their phones as they waited.

Once the group had loaded the last of Jake's equipment, they came back inside to continue their conversation about their weekend plans. I reached for my hiding place under the counter for my keys.

"Closing time," I hinted. Ok, it was more than a hint.

"Can we stay a little longer?" Betony pleaded. I tipped my head to the side, not sure she meant it. The rest of them said nothing, but their faces had the same pleading look hers did.

"And do what?" I asked, motioning to the empty seats. "The shop's closed."

"Show us your place," Betony said, nodding her head toward the swinging doors that led to my home. "We've never seen where you live. The outside of your house is so pretty. I'd love to see the inside."

"It's a *house*," I said, slightly exasperated, not knowing if their need to stay was more out of curiosity or wanting to avoid going home. I guessed it was the latter in Lorina's case. Probably Betony's as well.

"It's a *witch's* house," Betony persisted, her roundish cheeks rosy with a smile.

I rolled my eyes, resigned. "Fine."

The kids' shared a victory expression, and Lorina said, "Bet." For a moment, I thought she was talking to Betony, but then I remembered it was one of the slang expressions she'd taken to using. It was nice to see a sparkle in her eyes again.

"Not late, though," I said with a pointed finger. "It's not like I have snacks or video games or anything. It's not a hangout place." I wasn't kidding. What little time I didn't devote to the business or spellcasting side of Witch's Brew I typically spent on my couch reading. Well, it was a place for Hanna and Conall to hang out when they wanted to get away from their places, which was often. They were different, though.

"That's fine," Betony said. "We're just curious."

Shaking my head, I crossed the shop, locked the door, and motioned for them to follow me with a tilt of my head.

"Well, come on."

They trailed me through the swinging doors into the pantry/storage room that led to a second set of swinging doors into my kitchen, redolent with the fragrance of herbs that hung drying over the island in the center. Once the last visitor had crossed the threshold, I heard Cadence take in a soft gasp. And with good reason. My mother's kitchen was a work of art, and since I avoided cooking, it tended to stay that way.

Witch's Brew, where I spent eight to ten hours five days of the week, was in what used to be three large rooms: the parlor, sitting room, and dining room of an old Victorian house. The rest of it was my home. Three retrofitted rooms had the walls separating them removed and stood with new support beams. Now, the space held the shop and a sitting area where my customers enjoyed coffee and snacks. The only living space left on the bottom story was the back porch and my mother's kitchen, and I didn't share that space with just anyone.

My kitchen was massive, open, and sacrosanct. These kids did not know what a rare opportunity they had been given. A large, wood-topped butcher's block stood in the center. A Wedgewood cooking range that included both cooktops and multiple ovens below was centered on the far wall. A deep copper sink had been set into the countertop under an enormous window with a miniature herb garden inside the lip. Oregano, parsley, chives, and thyme grew in profusion there. Dried herbs hung from wood beams above the island crossing the center of the kitchen: lavender, sage. St. John's wort, olive leaf, juniper, calendula, and many more were wrapped in bundles and ready for spells or to be packaged for sale. The eclectic mix of subway tile, wood, and brick walls never struck me as odd until now. I suppose my kitchen appeared retro, given how modern kitchens looked nowadays with sleek granite countertops and brushed steel appliances. I never thought about it until seeing it through the eyes of these teens.

Their mouths fell open as they silently took it all in. After a few seconds, I started thinking this might have been a mistake. I knew it was unusual, but I'd never considered it jaw-dropping.

"This is *extra*," Lorina breathed, her wide brown eyes taking in the high ceiling before panning from wall to wall. A high compliment. She trod slowly to the right of the island, taking everything in with her unblinking gaze.

"Thank you." I relaxed a little. They were kids, but they were regulars, and... well, sort of *my* kids.

Betony strode through the room, her hand grazing the surface of the blue-gray countertop. Like Lorina, her observation swept over every feature, but she seemed reluctant to touch.

"What material is this?" she asked, pointing to the smooth countertop.

"Um... zinc," I replied. "It's one of the most suitable surfaces for banishing spells. Hanna bakes some of her healing foods on it—it helps with that, too. The copper sink is good for healing magic, or financial gain, as well as spells that need extra energy conducting."

Jake, for once, appeared small under the vaulted beams of my kitchen. He didn't know what to think until he finally spoke. "You're the real deal," he breathed. He dropped his gaze from the high ceiling and caught my bemused expression. "I mean—I kinda knew—"

"Don't mind Jake," Cadence chided, "He's a skeptic."

"I like *logic*," he explained, his hands expressive. "I just have a hard time..."

"Understanding?" I prodded. "Believing?" Jake signaled the affirmative with a shy, apologetic nod. I laughed softly. "That's OK. The craft is hard for some people to grasp, but that doesn't mean it doesn't work."

Betony had reached the center island, and her hand floated up to cradle a few drying lavender flowers in her palm. She then pulled her hand back as if shocked by an electric surge. "I'm sorry! Is that OK? Can I—?"

I held up a reassuring hand. "You're fine. If something wasn't OK to touch, I would have told you before you came in. This is a protected living space. Your energy now is that of curiosity and respect. You won't hurt them."

Her expression cleared, and a broad smile of small, straight teeth brightened her entire face. "Thank you! Yes, exactly. That's exactly how I feel."

Lorina and Betony crossed paths on the opposite side of the island. Cadence found the courage to leave Jake's side to explore as if my house was a museum and I had given them a free pass to see inside. Which, in a way, it was. I had hardly changed anything from the time my mother lived here. The entire room was almost like a time capsule to the era when Nora Blackwell lingered within the walls, brewing potions and baking goods blessed with herbs and sigils engraved into the crusts.

"You said you barely cook," Cadence began, "Why do you have such a gigantic kitchen like this? And where is your microwave?"

I laughed. "It's inside a cabinet. The kitchen was my mother's. She was a brown witch—a kitchen witch. You've seen my friend Hanna?"

"The pretty one with the long, brown hair that brings the food?" Jake replied. Cadence shot him a teasing side-eye, not surprised that he noticed but wanting to kid him a bit that he had. Cadence had been his sweetie since they were in 8th grade—an eternity in school years. Quick to smile but slow to open, she was still an enigma to me even after three years of coming into the store with the rest of the group.

"That's her. She's both a brown and a red witch." I avoided the topic of colors with most people outside of the coven. However, I believe in using teachable moments to help people understand the craft isn't dangerous.

"Is that uncommon? Being two types?" Betony asked.

"Very."

"You said brown is kitchen. What is red?"

"Love," I replied. "Hanna has an incredible ability to draw two perfect souls together."

"What type are you?" Lorina asked. Dang it. I'd walked into a trap of my own making. Everyone's eyes were on me now, waiting to hear how I answered.

"What about Conall?" Lorina inquired, sensing my discomfort. I silently blessed her for her swift intervention.

"He's orange, which, as you probably guessed, means he has the gift of prophecy."

"What about you?" Jake pressed.

"Gray," was all I replied, hoping they would drop it at that. Of course, they didn't.

Chapter 5

"What's a gray witch?" Betony asked. Well, judging from the way all of their eyes turned to me, they *all* wanted to know, but as usual, Betony, as so often was the case, spoke for the group.

I took a deep breath before replying, "Chaos witch." I tried to play it off as if it wasn't significant. That didn't work.

Four sets of eyebrows shot up in surprise. They had no clue what a chaos witch did, but anything with the word "chaos" in it dripped with anarchy, disarray, and tumult.

"Chaotic in D&D means a person who has no respect for rules," Lorina pointed out reluctantly, prodding me slowly but carefully, as if she'd discovered I had an oven for cooking children just her size. Leave it to the gamer to point that out.

I shook my head with a grave face. "I have great respect for rules. The laws of the craft demand it—at least in my case."

"What do you mean?" Betony had found the one bar-height chair I had tucked in a corner. She drew it near the butcher block and sat, her tiny feet swinging inches above the floor.

I moved to a more central kitchen location and took a position leaning against the counter near the copper sink.

"There are different types of craft," I began. "There is Wicca, which is a more earth and karma-based religion. They follow the rule of three—anything you do, good or bad, comes back to you three times."

"Are you Wiccan?" Betony asked.

My mouth flattened, hesitant to reply, knowing the answer only led to more questions. "No. I am a witch."

Lorina leaned her slim body over the butcher block and propped her long arms on it, dropping her head to her hands. For the millionth time, I wondered at her slenderness. How did she not crack a bone with every move? "What's the difference?"

"Witches don't have misgivings about curses and such. They believe that if person A did person B wrong, there is nothing wrong with cursing person A, and they have no fear of universal reprisal."

"No karma," Betony said. Her eyes had a shine to them as if the idea was delightful.

"And you're a chaos *witch?*" Funny how Jake, who moments ago had shaken off the notion that I was a pretender, was now concerned about my gray witch title combined with my craft's lack of fear of repercussion.

"I'm a little different," I conceded. "Being a gray witch comes at a price. Everything I touch, everything I do, runs a risk of leaving problems in its wake."

Betony frowned. "But your shop—"

"Is warded, remember?" I said with a pointed finger. "Strongly. So is my home. But if you notice, I barely leave it. Every time I step foot outside the bounds of protection, I risk harming the trajectory of someone's life. Including mine."

They were all silent.

"But your food—" Lorina started.

"Is delivered," I finished. "I order everything online."

"And your shop—" Cadence interjected.

"All the inventory ordered online and delivered by people who never see me unless it's through a window."

Betony sat back in her chair and drew her arms across her chest, obviously weirded out a bit by my agoraphobic lifestyle. "How do you… you know… see people?"

I shrugged. "I have Conall. And Hanna. My coven, sometimes. And my customers." I smiled and eyed each of them and realized that this small, ragtag group of teenage misfits were the closest I'd had to new guests, and new friends, in a long time.

☽○☾

They had questions, a million of them, dancing behind eyes that drank in every facet of my home, but all of them refrained. Instead, Cadence wandered over to the heavy wooden banister in the corner that curled upward into the rest of the house beyond.

"Can we… see more?" Her hand with its long and almond-shaped fingernails trailed up the banister, then back down. She gave me a tense smile.

It was either time to send them on their way or to open up more.

What the hell? They were kids, and they hadn't freaked out so far, and I was, to be honest, a little bored. Not to mention that Cadence rarely asked for anything. That she showed fascination was a little flattering.

"Onward." I gestured up the spiral staircase. Cadence's face, which had had a small smile before, widened into the beautiful grin I so rarely got to see, and I regretted nothing.

We wound our way up to the second-story hallway, where they could see the wood-framed doorways to each room. Every space had walnut floors, except for the white-tiled bathroom, the furniture in keeping with the Victorian home style. The architect had intended for the upper four chambers to be bedrooms of differing sizes. Since I was the only resident, and my business took up the rest of the living space, they had instead become a master bedroom, a small den, a study/library, and a guest room. The single upstairs bathroom was centrally located, and since it was also the only room with light-colored walls and floor, it was also the only room they could see well without turning on a light. Bright moonlight reflected enough through the window to show the room's antique features.

The kids paused at the top of the stairs as if reluctant to explore.

"This is your—your home," Lorina said. Her tone was so reverent that I wasn't sure how to respond, and I felt a tiny bit awkward.

"You're my guests," I shrugged. "Come on. There isn't much to it." I turned to the right and led them into the guest bedroom—the most boring room in the house. Cast iron bed with a white spread. A small white desk tucked into a corner beside a tiny white chest of drawers and a slender mirror. The kids reviewed the contents with obvious disappointment, which was what I was hoping for. Conall and Hanna had stayed in the room often, (not at the same time,) but that wouldn't mean much to them. I didn't want to think every single corner of my life harbored mystic secrets and spells.

For that, I took them to my study.

The house didn't have many rooms, but what it lacked in quantity it made up for in size. The rooms downstairs made for a comfortably large shop, and my study upstairs was more extensive than standard living rooms. Thick burgundy curtains framed three floor-to-ceiling windows, which I used to block out any trace of sunlight when the need arose. Bookshelves lined walls made from the same wood as the floor and stretched from floor to ceiling. Books filled every shelf, kept safe behind glass-fronted cupboards. A slender ladder allowed me to reach some of the topmost volumes. Each work had been written, at the least, decades before and held centuries of knowledge. I had read them all and had committed as much as I could to memory. One of the benefits of homeschooling with LaDonna—lots and *lots* of reading.

A desk built into the wall had a draw-down door hiding the many inner shelves that held my personal supply of spell crafting goods. In the center of the room, a matching table held my private crafting equipment: my athame, my book of shadows, and a small altar devoted to the only otherworldly spirit I sensed any connection to, Baron Samedi. A wooden pedestal next to the table held my favorite spell book: my mother's book of shadows. Other tools included my crystal ball, thick candles on stands set at the compass points through the room, and a silver chalice with a pentagram engraved on it.

"This room is a do-not-touch room," I said sternly as they crossed the threshold, but I could tell the caution was unnecessary. Their eyes darted everywhere, from the multicolored book spines to the stained-glass window casting a technicolor tree of life onto the table, but they showed no sign of trespassing on my private items.

"What *is* this place?" Betony's voice showed how well she sensed the power that emitted from every corner of the room. Her hands danced up and down, caressing the energy, and I smiled a small half-smile. Leave it to Betony to appreciate what an average human would not.

"This is what I call my room of power."

"What is that?"

I paused, unsure how to explain it adequately, especially to kids unfamiliar with the craft. "You know how I told you that I bless everything that comes through the store with a protection spell?" Four heads bobbed up and down. "That blessing spell… it's almost routine. Do you understand?"

Jake and Cadence nodded, but Betony and Lorina gave no sign they followed along. "It's rote. It's… I do it all the time. I don't put much effort into it. It's mostly a precaution. Because of who I am. *What* I am."

"You're protecting them from your chaos witch-ness," Jake concluded.

"Exactly. And besides, once it's in their hands and they walk out the door, they imbue the items with their personal energy. My concern is to make sure that whatever they buy is a blank slate when they leave. Nothing negative." *Nothing Murphy*, I added to myself.

"Here… this is different. This is where I can channel myself fully. It's my sanctuary." I didn't care to explain any further, to describe how when I was in my element, the wind blew indoors, the sun or moon and stars shone through the ceiling, and the power of the universe sparked at my fingertips. They didn't need to hear that part.

Betony's fingers hovered an inch away from one of the bookshelves. *"Handfasting and Love Magick… Celebrating the Pagan Calendar…*

Hexes and Jinxes! Ooh, can I read some of these?"

Before I could answer, a black shadow darted through the doorframe, scuttled under the desk, and emerged atop the table. It stretched its slender legs, twitched its tail, and regarded the group with disdain that only an eight-pound feline familiar could.

"Kitty!" Betony squealed, the books forgotten. Well, that's not exactly accurate. It sounded more like, "Keee!"

"That's Rex," I said by introduction. "He's my familiar and—be careful. He's a cranky old man."

"He doesn't look old," Betony remarked. And he didn't, but Rex had come into my life when I was about five, which meant that he was at the very least twenty-one years old. If he resembled any other familiar, he'd be with me until I no longer needed him or another came to take his place. I had an unbreakable bond with the cantankerous feline; I could imagine my grumpy, old, beautiful black boy staying with me until I died. That he had come out now told me he'd discerned something I hadn't foreseen yet. If that weren't true, he wouldn't have deigned to bless them with his presence.

Lorina, who had extended her hand above Rex's black, shiny head, froze in place to give Rex a chance to decide how he'd respond. Rex regarded her momentarily before arching his head and back so she could stroke his fur.

"You're unusual," I said with uncommon admiration. "He rarely reaches out to others. Normally, he makes them come to him. But be careful. His affection sometimes doesn't last. He'll strike out before long." Which was true. Rex had absolute devotion to me, but he allowed himself an occasional pet from a stranger.

Lorina gave my furry boy a couple more strokes before she stepped aside so Betony could stretch out to pet Rex. Rex, however, was having none of it. His lean paw stretched out and swatted at her before she touched him, and his bright green eyes regarded her with nothing less than detestation.

"Oh!" Betony snatched her hand close to her body in surprise. I flinched in sympathy. Usually, Rex gave people at least a moment to admire him before displaying any sign that he wasn't interested in further affection. It was unheard of for him not to let someone admire him for at least a moment. And he never eyed them with contempt the way he glared at Betony.

"Rex!" I admonished, but Rex stepped into a moonbeam and flopped on his side atop the table, sending stained-glass technicolor reflections across himself. He began grooming the fur on his side as if he had done nothing wrong at all.

"I'm sorry," I said apologetically. "He's not usually like that." And while I didn't like the idea that Rex had acted that way toward a guest, part of me wasn't sorry. It was curious. Rex had excellent instincts. What had he sensed that I hadn't?

"It's OK," Betony murmured, but I could tell it wasn't. Her off-put face with its downturned mouth clarified that she was unhappy that my familiar had not cared for her.

☽○☾

"There are a couple of more rooms," I said, "But they're pretty normal."

Jake shrugged. But he'd read Betony's expression as much as I had and wanted to distract her from her disappointment. "Let's see it."

I steered myself to the front of the group and led them to my bedroom. My favorite parts were a white handmade spread and the two fat velvet chairs flanking a collapsible table in front of a curved bay window overlooking Oberon Street. A small dressing room at the far end of the room made up for the lack of space.

My cozy den was situated across the hall, the only room not done up in Victorian to match the home's exterior. Bookshelves ran from floor to ceiling. On the window ledge, a statue of Hestia, goddess of the home, stood balanced between watching the street below and keeping an eye on the room. An enormous, brightly painted canvas of Papa Legba brightened up the walls. The plush loveseat served as my couch, and three chairs with blankets across the backs made the space cozy.

"No TV?" Lorina asked.

"Uh, yeah. It's…" I crossed the room and opened a set of cupboard doors, sliding them into the wall to reveal a medium-sized TV set. It had a light coating of dust. I'm not a big Netflixer.

"You like to hide your electronics," Cadence observed. I shrugged. I'd never thought of it that way, but I supposed she was right. The modern equipment didn't give the house the antique appearance I preferred.

"This is the coolest house," Lorina breathed.

Now the tour had concluded, the room grew silent. They acted in no rush to leave, and I had no reason to show them to the door, other than I had nothing to say and was a creature of habit longing to put on my pajamas.

"What do you do after work, usually?" Betony asked.

I scoffed. "Read a book. Text with Hanna or Conall. Order dinner, if I'm hungry."

"We could do that," she offered. "The last part, I mean."

"Y'all have been snacking all night," I laughed.

Jake grinned. "I can always eat."

"Anyone want to chip in on pizza?" Betony asked everyone. Heads bobbed up and down. Oh, to have the metabolism of a teenager again.

I collected some cash, decisions were made, and I called in an order for pepperoni pizza and a 2-liter of soda.

That done, an odd silence fell over the group again as they settled into the chairs around the living room to wait. When I saw them at my shop, they behaved like chatterboxes full of inside jokes, rambling stories, and sharing memes on their phones. My shop had become their second home. Tonight, I was an outlier—the token accepted adult in a tight-knit group of friends. They liked me, but their knowledge of me was limited to what I shared within the walls of Witch's Brew downstairs. They had always seen me as the Witch of Gryphon, but now they knew it wasn't a façade I presented to the world as a novelty. I lived the craft, both in the shop and in my home.

I was a for-real-no-kidding witch, and Betony, for one, wasn't about to stop her inquiries. "Have you ever played with a Ouija board?"

"Sure," I shrugged, "They can be useful, but remember to think of it as a tool, not a toy. I have a Mystic Spiral, too. Those are easier to use alone, I think."

"What's a Mystic Spiral?"

I headed to a cabinet next to the television where I stored my games and opened the doors wide. A few games were everyday items you'd find in any superstore shelf—card games, board games, and the like. Others were more on the occult side, many of them wooden boxes with symbols or scripts on the side mixed in with the more commonly recognized heavy cardboard. One game was an embossed leather scroll rolled tight with a slender strip of latigo. Velvet drawstring bags held playing pieces such as marbles, but a few had spilled out. Toward the front of the jumbled shelf stood a pewter cat that resembled Rex and a carved wooden werewolf.

Jake had stood up from the couch, prepared to lend a hand if needed. He surveyed the cabinet's contents and accepted the box with the Mystic Spiral in it as I handed it to him.

"Cool games," he noted.

"Some of them are old ones handed down from my mother's family," I explained as I shut the cabinet doors.

"Where do you want to play?" Betony asked, standing. "In your power room?"

The others followed suit, standing and looking for direction.

"Let me get a couple of things from my study, and we'll set up downstairs," I said. "We can pull tables together so everyone can sit comfortably and see the board."

Although Betony's slight pout suggested her disappointment, she didn't argue. I quickly gathered two black pillar candles and brass stands from the other room and a pack of wooden matches, and we trooped downstairs.

Chapter 6

A few minutes later, we had two mismatched tables of similar heights pushed together covered by one of the few dusty tablecloths I stashed in case I hosted a Lughaidh coven meeting inside Witch's Brew. On a nearby table lay a pepperoni pizza, which had arrived in record time. In the center, we unfolded the Mystic Spiral board, and I aligned the north, south, east, and west indicators in the proper direction. The Spiral, in case you've never used one, is like a Ouija board on steroids. Nearly twice as big, the board holds letters and numbers and rings of zodiac signs, colors, planets, pictures, and a handful of complete words. In the corners, symbols represented the four elements and compass points.

I handed Candace the booklet that described the different icons on the board for anyone who needed something explained. When everyone settled into their places and grew quiet, I lit an incense stick to help conduct the proper energies between our world and the veil beyond.

"Who wants to go first?" I asked.

"What's this?" Lorina fingered a few grains of Alabama red clay in the bottom of the Mystic Spiral box with the hand not holding the last few bites of her dinner.

"Graveyard dirt," I said.

"Grave—what?"

I let out a quick laugh. "Graveyard dirt. From my mother's grave. For protection."

Lorina snatched her hand from the box and brushed her fingers together to remove the remnants of red dust from her fingertips. I held out a hand to reassure her. "It's fine, I promise. There is no harm in touching it. It's okay."

Lorina didn't look too convinced, but she also didn't run to the nearest sink to wash her hand off, either.

I took the matches and faced the candle nearest to me. Closing my eyes, I sent out a quick, unspoken spell to lower the protection on the perimeter of my property a tad so I could open the door to positive energies—and only positive energies.

Loving spirits, gather round,
My wards to only you are downed
Flame of fire, flame of light,
Guide us with the second sight,
All harmful souls from here must flee,
And as I will, so mote it be.

"Who goes first?" Betony asked.

I sent feelers into the Universe to see what the surrounding energies led me to, but before I voiced an answer, Betony said, "Me and Lorina. Come on, Lorina."

Not the impression I received, but OK, I thought. It wouldn't hurt anything. The answers wouldn't be as strong from energy not already nearby, but if that was what Betony wanted to do, I didn't sense any harm in it, either.

Betony and Lorina sat across the table from one another, and the rest of us leaned in to have a better view of the board. Cadence ran a finger's edge along the slender instruction book in her hand, but I could have told her she wouldn't need it. Hanna and I had played this game until I learned the book frontward and backward. Still, it never hurt to have a person verify an impression.

"What do we do?" Betony asked.

"Take the circle and rest your fingers on it," I instructed. Lorina took the clear circle planchette and placed it in the center of the board. The two of them put the tips of their fingers on the edges, Lorina's hand spindly like spider legs, Betony's soft with short digits.

"It's like a Ouija planchette," I said. Two sets of blank eyes met mine. Neither had used a Ouija board, either.

"Don't press hard," I told them. "Just barely touch it. You want enough energy to come from your body to harness enough power to slide the piece, but not enough to influence which direction it goes. And don't cover the center of the planchette; you'll want to read the answers."

The room grew quiet, and nothing happened for several seconds. An energy came into the room like a gentle breeze. Perhaps this was it.

Lorina opened her mouth and said, "Maybe—"

And the piece skittered timidly across the board, and I smiled.

"E… C…" Betony followed the piece as it danced around the board.

I needed to show governance over the conversation before it went too deep and the spirit got lost trying to spell its way around the circle. "Hi," I said in greeting.

The piece only paused for a second before it flew across the board to a word.

Hello.

"Whoa." Lorina's eyes became enormous, brown circles.

Betony laughed, delighted but also astonished. "God, I thought it was going to fly out from under my fingers!"

"Me too," Lorina agreed with a hesitant laugh. She swallowed visibly, and her fingers trembled a bit over the planchette.

I addressed the board. "How are you?"

The circular planchette moved from letter to letter. O… K.

"Ok," Bet said. "Cool. Who are you?" Her voice was eager as if she was hoping for a particular answer. I hoped it didn't influence her sway on the piece under her fingers.

Slight pause. Then a movement to the word GO and the symbol for Pisces.

Brows furrowed around the table, but I knew not to read too much into this right away.

"Anyone know a Pisces who died?" Betony asked.

"It'd be someone with a birthday between February 19th and March 20th," I added, in case it helped. I didn't think it would. That the zodiac symbol preceded the word ''go'' took away from the symbology of the Pisces symbol. And it didn't have to be someone who died, either. Some entities had never existed other than as a spirit—some think of them as angels, demons, or guides. Still, I let Betony run with it. I'd been wrong on occasion, and after all, this conversation had only begun. I might have read too much into it. Perhaps Betony had her finger on the pulse of this energy better than I did since she held the planchette. She'd already shown an inclination to spiritual divination. And I was trying to be hands off in this session to test their abilities and see what energies they drew.

No one had an answer about what Pisces person might be trying to connect with them. The circular planchette grew still. Then it went back again. And again.

Go… Pisces. Go… Pisces.

"Go Fish?" I offered. Lorina's hand, which had been lightly resting on the piece as it danced across the board, dropped to the table.

"Could that be it?" she asked, incredulous.

I shrugged. "It's possible. Sometimes the spirits get creative to make the message short, like using emojis. It's funny, though. Most times, it doesn't work."

"Go Fish," Lorina breathed. Her hand withdrew from the planchette as she sat back in her chair. "My grandmother and I used to play that all the time."

"She wants to talk to you!" Betony squealed. "Put your hand back! Ooh, I wonder if my grandmother will try to reach me!"

Lorina bolted upright and slapped her hand back on the piece.

"Lightly!" I directed. Lorina's hand came up a bit as her slender fingers rested delicately over the place where *SPIRAL* was etched into the thin glass in silver foil. The planchette stuttered over to a word.

HELLO.

"Gramma?" Lorina asked, her voice wavering on acceptance but still reluctant.

Go… Pisces.

"Go Fish?" Lorina whispered. The planchette traveled in a wide arch before it rested on its word of choice.

YES.

A tremor crept into Lorina's voice. "Is your name Julia?"

YES.

Determined to remain skeptical, Lorina pulled her hand from the piece and held her hands up, fingers splayed.

"Someone else do this," she pleaded. "Maybe I'm moving the piece and don't realize it."

Jake slid into the seat across from Betony and placed his hand on the planchette as Lorina slid into the chair Jake had emptied as if she had no bones in her tall body.

"Lightly," Betony commanded Jake, her eyes like sparks.

"I know, I know," Jake said, but I noticed him lifting his fingers off the piece slightly at her reproach.

Lorina, still enthralled with the answers she'd received so far, leaned in, ready to ask more questions.

"What… what is your last name?"

The piece hesitated for a moment before dancing across the board.

E…. M… E…

"Emergency?" Betony guessed.

I shook my head, the name already conveyed to me. "Emerson."

Lorina melted into her chair like a popsicle in the summer heat and waved at herself with her hand. Cadence handed her the booklet from inside the game, and Lorina used it as a fan. "Emerson. Oh my god."

"Is that right?" Betony asked, as if Lorina's body language hadn't already said everything.

A rapping at the door shook us out of the spell the board had cast. Any energy present evaporated at the sound. Every eye in the room turned to the women behind the oval on the storefront glass. One was Hanna, a meager smile on her tanned face framed with layers of hair the color of tiger's eye. The other was also unmistakable. Long hair the color of cherry Coca-Cola. Mediterranean olive skin. Eyes the shade of pine trees in a misty forest. Why was she here at this late hour? It made no sense.

"Who is that with Hanna?" Betony asked.

I didn't answer at first. I rose from my chair to open the door, partly out of habit, the other half out of respect. The women on the other side crossed with different bearings—LaDonna strode in, a wave of power in her wake. The moment she crossed the threshold, the power of every object inside Witch's Brew grew tenfold. Hanna followed her as if on a leash. And speaking of on a leash, a small dog trailed my friend. I'd never seen anything like it—as if a corgi and a wolf had made a puppy, and it was the cutest thing I had seen in days. The pup had no clue about the energy in the room—he trotted from person to person, happy to have people paying attention to him. He propped his front paws—fat little feet for his little body size—on Jake's leg. Jake grinned despite himself and bent down to give the dog scratches under his collar.

All eyes were on us, although I wished they weren't. It was unheard of for me to host guests other than Hanna and Conall at this hour. And here we were, me and a handful of teenagers harnessing the power of the Spiral. I felt like a teenager myself, caught in naughty behavior by a concerned parent.

"LaDonna, Hanna," I motioned to the table, "This is Betony, Lorina, Jake, and Cadence. Y'all, know Hanna from the store. This is LaDonna Whelen, high priestess of the Lughaidh coven."

Chapter 7

It was as if the air in the room became supercharged. The power that LaDonna brought with her was undeniable. The teens in the room sat back in their chairs and absorbed her presence. It was a lot to take in.

LaDonna Whelen has always been in my life. Some kids had Santa Claus to keep them from misbehaving, and others had Jesus. I had La-Donna.

It was she who pushed me through home school after my mother died and convinced me to take some business courses at the local college. She had held the trust of my mother's estate to hand over to me when I turned eighteen. She made sure I always had a home within the coven, no matter how standoffish I kept myself. She was also why I had the building we stood in today, the home I'd had with my mother, a bed-and-breakfast once called Blackwell Lodge. Using her local notoriety and networking skills to help an inexperienced eighteen-year-old busi-nesswoman build a metaphysical shop out of an oversized Victorian house (in the middle of Alabama, no less) was nothing to LaDonna.

Thanks to hard work—and tons of spells—Witch's Brew and I had both prospered. Not only prospered, but I had never known hunger, and at twenty-six, had already started on my retirement and had a comfort-able rainy-day fund, just in case. For that, I was grateful. Astrologically, I am a Cancer. We like our security.

LaDonna didn't judge me; that wasn't in her nature. Hanna, either. However, the energy in the room was off somehow now that they were here—unseen forces somehow engaged in a tug-of-war.

That's when I noticed how Betony watched LaDonna. She had stood and pulled all sixty-four inches of her body to its full height and had her lips slightly turned into a smile as if she was preparing to take a selfie—modeling for an audience. My surrogate mother wasn't tall—five foot five at the tallest. Somehow, she'd always struck me as towering.

"Nice to meet you," LaDonna said, her voice low and husky for a woman, and her accent more central United States than one typically finds in Gryphon, although she'd lived here her whole life. Southern accents ran thick as kudzu here. It was also, I recognized once I reached maturity, sexy, as was her curvy figure. There was a reason that men were happy she led the coven when they observed spring rites. But that's another story.

"You're the high priestess?" Betony asked. Her tone held an odd bal-ance of reverence and misgiving, confusion whether to speak to her as an average human or if she should follow up her sentences with "your majesty."

"I am," LaDonna replied. Damn, she could even make two words sound regal without sounding pompous. How did she do that?

"Do you... how does that work? I mean—if you can tell me."

LaDonna breathed a laugh that managed to be both amused and friendly. "I assumed the role by a collective vote of the coven."

"You're democratic."

"Oh, yes. The power of the coven would never work if it didn't function in collective harmony. Conflict can ruin the group dynamic. I needed to have the complete confidence of all the members."

"How many are there?"

"Twelve regular members, including Hanna here, and Conall as well, and their fathers, and others," LaDonna said. "When Murphy joins us, we have thirteen."

"Is that normal? Or a lot? Or..."

"It's common. Both twelve and thirteen are magic numbers."

"Wow."

"Yes," she said with a dip of her head. "And while it was wonderful to meet you all, we must speak to Murphy in private."

The other three youths had already started gathering their backpacks and phones in preparation to go. Betony hadn't noticed—or was acting as if she hadn't.

"Does this have to do with the robber?"

On the one hand, I was proud of Betony. I would never have had the initiative to speak to LaDonna so succinctly so soon after meeting her. Even when I lived with her and spent every day and night with her, the power she radiated intimidated me. Part of me was appalled. LaDonna had asked to speak to me in private. You don't tread into a setting not intended for you like that. When the coven leader says "in private," you go.

"It's for us to discuss with Murphy," LaDonna said with another slight motion of her head. "If she decides to discuss it with you later, I will leave that up to her."

Placated but not satisfied, Betony gathered her belongings with the rest of the group and headed toward the door. To my surprise, I received huge hugs from all the young women before they headed out, and even Jake gave me an awkward side embrace. They had never done that before, perhaps because their visits were during business hours.

The four of them each offered a quiet "Bye" at the door. I locked it behind them but left the outside light on so they could see themselves safely across the veranda and down the stairs. Then I turned to face La-Donna and Hanna. And the dog. What was the deal with the dog? Neither of them had one before.

I cleared my throat and pressed my hands together, wove the fingers. "Would either of you like a drink? Coffee, water, sweet tea, soda…?

"Hot tea, if you have it," LaDonna said. "Chamomile?"

"That sounds good," Hanna agreed. "I'll have the same."

"Of course," I replied. Their request made me concerned: chamomile encourages relaxation and reduces stress. What was bothering them? I mean, Hanna wandered in and out of my house as if it was her own, Conall too, and was welcome to do so. Tonight, she followed LaDonna in a coven role, that was clear. It was unheard of for LaDonna to come calling at this hour unless it was for coven purposes, like a moonlight ritual.

I invited them into the kitchen and prepared cups of tea for the three of us. We made small talk about the herbs in the windowsill and the lives of other coven members, how they were doing, their jobs, their children. I learned the dog's name was Oswald, but that he was called Rolf. The name sounded vaguely familiar, but I couldn't place why, and neither of them said they had an answer. Hanna leaned against the counter nearest to me, and LaDonna took the barstool at the island that Betony had emptied earlier that evening as I prepared our tea. Once I had served us all and the Rolf had laid down on the floor with his little wolfy head on his paws, I propped myself against the kitchen counter across the island from LaDonna.

"OK, what's up? You never come calling at this hour. I'm guessing it's not an emergency, or you wouldn't have waited to tell me why you're here."

LaDonna blew across the top of her mug and took a quick sip of the hot brew. "No, it's not an emergency, but it is urgent. Luke sensed you needed us tonight, and so I came." Luke was LaDonna's significant other of over two decades. He was a prophetic witch, an orange like Conall. "Tell me about the robber, your… friend? mentioned earlier."

I related the incident from earlier that evening, trying not to leave out any details she might find relevant. Her dark green eyes studied me as I spoke but didn't evaluate me—it was more like an assessment. LaDonna perceived the importance of every nuance of energy I emitted—body posture, vocal tone, the power I displayed. She would use this and the information she received from the Universe (she called it the Source) to decide what applied to… well, to whatever was going on.

I ended my story with my concern about the robber's ability to cross into the protected realm of Witch's Brew. "Is it possible the wards aren't working?"

"Possible, but not likely."

"Well then, how?"

During our exchange, Hanna took a seat on the tile floor next to Rolf and scratched him behind his ears. It was obvious she had no plan to interrupt whatever LaDonna had to say. LaDonna's mouth flattened into that unsettled line I rarely saw. "There is a chance there is a power stronger than the wards. I've always told you that you are more powerful than you know."

I shook my head. "Yeah. You've told me that my whole life. And I have always tried to protect the world and myself from the chaos I cause whenever I leave here. I never leave the shop anymore. I order my groceries and everything else I need from the internet. I'm basically self-quarantined."

"There is one thing that, in theory, could compound the power you already have. Like a lightning rod amplifying your power and theirs."

The strength faded from my spine as dismay washed over me. "No way. There's a way to make my chaos *worse?* No! What? *Who?* What could possibly make chaos witch power worse?"

LaDonna paused, as if she hated to say. "Another chaos witch."

Chapter 8

Well, damn. This entire day had gone from awful to unusual to more dreadful than being held at gunpoint. Hell, I'd welcome the gunman right back into my shop and hand him everything I had if I could get LaDonna to take back what she'd just said. My grip on my mug had loosened, and I caught it before it slipped from my trembling hands. The bottom of the ceramic cup ticked rapidly on the zinc countertop at my fingertips as I set the cup down onto the counter.

Parts of my past coursed through my mind—a string of damages I'd caused, too many to count. I tried to rein in my power, but over the years, it grew larger than I could hold back, and like a dam damaged by weeks—months—of pouring rain, the destruction would happen. I never wanted it. (Well, that's not entirely true. A couple of times, I caused a little *push* in the—right? wrong?—direction when karma needed a little hand.)

Arguments… car accidents… illnesses… floods… money problems… storms… things breaking, falling, catching fire, getting lost, dying… always, always, always *when I was around.*

"I thought…. We were… rare."

LaDonna nodded. "You are. A chaos witch only comes around possibly once every twenty-five generations." My brain did the math quickly. Once every 500 years, roughly.

"Then how?" My voice pleaded for understanding as my gaze flicked from LaDonna to Hanna and back. LaDonna took in a deep breath and paused before making sure I was watching her when she responded.

"There is a chance you may not be the chaos witch we have always thought you were."

I sputtered, incredulous. "Not a chaos witch? LaDonna, have you *seen* my life? There's no way—"

She held up a palm in my direction, and I stopped. Her forest green eyes regarded me with care. "When did you realize you were a chaos witch?"

I scoffed and started pacing the strip of floor across from her, cautious not to step on Rolf as I walked. "When everything in my life turned to shit."

"And when did that happen?"

"When…" I threw up my hands, both saddened and angry. "LaDonna, you *know* when."

"When do you recall?" she stressed.

I stopped pacing. If I'd had it in me to glare at the high priestess, I would have. "When Mom died. When *all* our moms died. Hanna. Me. Conall." My hands waved in uncharacteristically broad motions as I spoke.

"And how old were you?"

"Ten."

She nodded, and her gaze flicked to the door for a moment as if she was checking to make sure no one was listening. Of course, no one was.

"What are you getting at, LaDonna?"

"How much of your life do you remember before she passed away?" Hanna asked. She had been silent for so long, and the question was so unexpected, she caught me off guard.

Most of the memories I had of life before my mother's death were... well, were of her. Her presence was a constant in every corner of my life. Nora Blackwell hadn't just been my mother. She'd been my best friend and the guardian who had kept the world warded against the damaging effects of my "grayness."

"Not a lot," I admitted. "Most of my memories are of my mother."

The high priestess nodded. "I remember a lot, Murphy. I remember a beautiful child with a radiant smile who drew everyone to her and who had grace and charm no one could resist."

Hanna nodded. "That's what I remember, too. You were so outgoing, and you always smiled."

Grace? Smiles? Me? "But why the bad luck, then?"

"It didn't start until after your mother's death," Hanna said.

"Because her wards wore off."

LaDonna shook her head. "I don't think that's it."

"But my school burned down!" I argued.

"Sometimes schools burn."

"The tornado—"

"It's Alabama, Murphy. There are always tornadoes."

"The curse—"

"Said a gray would *come unto* your family, not *into* your family. That only means 'to.' It said nothing about birth."

My mouth flapped, but I was running out of arguments. My mind spun with the possibilities. Me, not a gray?

"If I'm not a gray, then *what the hell am I?*"

"You are a powerful witch whose energies went a little crazy when a gray witch arrived in Gryphon."

"When I turned ten." My mind was clicking now. "If she was a new-born baby, then that would make her…"

"Sixteen," LaDonna confirmed. "Much like your new inquisitive friend."

One name echoed in my head like a thunderclap. Betony.

Oh, shit.

Chapter 9

Betony. Now all of her break-ups, her inability to control her emotions, her family tree and its multiple confusing broken branches, her getting hit by a car at thirteen, and her need to self-medicate were starting to make sense. Tumbling the notion in my head, I pulled the thread further. Whenever she went to stay with an older sibling, a catastrophe befell her family, driving her back to her parents' house. She was constantly getting into fights at school—verbal and physical. Cars always broke down around her. Story after story after story came back to me. I'd always chalked it up to her need to embellish for attention. Could she be the gray, and not me?

It was my turn to peek over the double doors to make sure none of the teens who had left were lingering. The meaning of the tarot reading was falling into place now. The high priestess card didn't mean my mother—it meant my actual high priestess, and LaDonna was also the insightful person the spread had shown. Betony was my eager student, but she was also the soldier coming home—the familial love and devotion card. The last card, meaning unexpected or unfortunate arrival of something, made a lot more sense now—it showed how I'd have to explain to Betony that her life would be that of a gray witch. Talk about bad news.

Bad news? Try the worst! If LaDonna was right, the nasty events that tailed me had only been secondhand gray energy affecting my life. What will it be like knowing that she has that—and worse—to look forward to forever? At the moment, she had hope that one day, she'd leave home and her misfortune would end. I remembered how miserable chaos energy was to shoulder at sixteen, and my heart ached for her.

How on earth was I supposed to divert this future from coming true? There was no way I could teach Betony *not* to be a chaos witch. I might as well ask her to change her blood type.

One mystery from the reading remained: who was going to lie and deceive me?

"What do I do? Is there a way to fix this?" I asked, my voice pleading.

"What would you fix?" LaDonna asked. "The Universe brings things into being when they are meant to be. If there is a gray witch in the world now, it is because the world needed a gray."

"But grays are *terrible*," I insisted. "They wreck everything!"

"They are chaos witches," LaDonna reprimanded, her raspy voice stern, "and are part of the universal structure. You're familiar with the idea of chaos theory?"

I scoffed. "Yeah, of course. How could I *not* be?"

"Tell me the way you understand it."

I paused. It had been so long since I'd tried to define it, and I had to think. "It means something that affects a string of events that would otherwise be… deterministic. Predictable. Chaos theory means that one little change can make them not predictable."

"Not *as* predictable," LaDonna corrected. "But there is still a design that forms in time."

"Oh yeah… that… um…"

"Deterministic chaos," Hanna chimed in. "Unpredictable, but there is a pattern." Leave it to my best friend to remember that.

"A useless pattern for being a chaos witch," I muttered. "I mean, it's not like life can be calculated like weather patterns or—or population dynamics."

"Not to us," LaDonna said. "But the Universe has a much bigger view of those patterns."

I slumped against the counter. "You can't really think humans can be reduced to predictable math, or some sort of equation."

LaDonna's eyebrows raised. "I think there is a much closer link to science, math, and magic than humankind has ever supposed."

Now my mouth mimicked the flat line LaDonna had made moments before.

Witchcraft is a diverse religion and follows several paths. Unlike many religions, which have doctrine treated like law, witchcraft is less rigid. Certain witches are adamant about using specific candle colors, precise fragrances, and uttering exact incantations. Other witches can turn actions as simple as drinking a cup of coffee into a day-starting ritual and can use a birthday candle with as much effectiveness as an anointed ritual one. I fall into the latter category, except for spells that I wished to imbue with substantial power. The beauty and solemnity of ritual heightens my power spells.

Whether one harnesses power—or the Source—LaDonna told me it all comes down to energy. The same energy force found in the particles that compose all matter powered our spells. Or so LaDonna had taught me when I was her foster daughter. I still remember the candlelight reflecting off her face as she sprinkled salt around the perimeter of our circle on the concrete patio behind her home. The smell of the surrounding garden was as intoxicating as her chant.

She taught me that while some called their deity God, others Jehovah, others Allah, she called on various deities and worshiped the Mother Goddess and the Horned God as archetypes to which she directed her attention. She taught me not to believe in them per se, but to believe in the power and the ideas they represent and to use that power to fuel my spells. Where attention goes, energy flows.

"You think this is all… some master Universal plan? And I may not be a chaos witch, but Betony might be? If I'm not, what would I be?"

LaDonna regarded me with a strange combination of both concern and admiration. "Murphy, I think you may be all the colors of the prism and then some."

☽◯☾

I sat on the floor. Well, that's not exactly true. My legs gave out, and I found myself in a puddle on the tile. Rolf trotted over to me, and I scratched under his collar as he gave me a wolfy smile.

Hanna slid to my side, put a tanned, toned arm around my shoulders, and rested her head against mine. She smelled, as usual, like the honeysuckle essential oil she used.

"When did you get a dog?" I asked, desperate to change the subject.

"I didn't," she said as Rolf sidled up against her and smiled an adorable doggy smile. She scratched his fuzzy head and returned his smile.

"Whose is he?"

"Yours, sort of," she replied. My brow furrowed. How could a dog be "sort of" mine? And why the hell was she giving me a dog?

"You came here with LaDonna knowing I'd have all of this dumped on me, and now you want me to foster a dog?"

LaDonna stood and crossed the short distance between us. Hanna pulled her enormous purse to her side, drew out a purple bath towel, and laid it on the floor. I partly expected Rolf to piddle on it. Still, from the commanding way that LaDonna moved toward us, something significant was about to happen that did not involve focused urination.

The priestess leaned over Rolf, put her hand on top of his head, and whispered, "*Forma restituet.*"

Hanna scooted away from the dog, and I followed suit. The energy in the air grew as thick as after summer rain, and a gentle haze formed around the edges of Rolf's soft fur. The dog's coat grew taught as his skin expanded and the surrounding aura rippled into blue tones I knew well.

No way. No way!

My jaw tightened as I retreated another few paces, scrabbling backward in a crab walk. Although I implicitly trusted my priestess and my best friend, I couldn't help but break out in a light sweat as what was a dog only moments before contorted and expanded. The knees thickened and changed direction, and the paws become long, thin fingers. The sable hair shed to the floor and dissolved into nothingness, except for that on his head, which thickened and grew dark and wavy. A muscular hand reached down for the towel to cover the more manly parts that were developing. The canine muzzle withdrew into a homo sapiens mouth as the face developed into oblong, tanned skin and brown eyes so deep they were almost black.

Conall.

If I could have turned into more of a puddle on the floor, I would have. Instead, I leaned on the island cabinets behind me as if my spine had slid out of my backside.

"How... no, wait. *Why?"*

"You need help," Hanna said as LaDonna withdrew a glass from my cabinet and filled it with water for Conall, who accepted it gratefully and took an enormous swallow. She also pulled out the bottle of Prosecco and poured the rest of us a small glass each. I took mine with a grateful smile, wishing I could chug the wine as Conall had his water.

"The coven and I will continue to do our part with you to protect your store and your home," Hanna continued. "But—"

"But I can see ahead where others can't," Conall finished his melodious, masculine timbre as heartening as usual. I think half of the reason Conall had the success he did at reading was because women loved to hear him talk. He tied the terrycloth around his narrow waist and sat on the floor carefully so as not to expose himself. "Rolf and I can keep you safe if I foresee a danger that others don't."

I wanted to argue. I wanted to remind them that nobody could foresee the future in my protected realm as well as I did. But I also couldn't distance myself from my own life and separate my feelings from my wishes the way Conall would. If Betony was the gray and she tried to hurt or manipulate me, it was likely Conall would see my path far more clearly than I would. If she wasn't, he'd have a better line on that as well.

"You are going to hide here as a dog?" I asked weakly. "Why would you do that?"

Conall shrugged. "You're my best friend," he said. After a beat, he faced Hanna with a guilty expression. "And you, too, of course.

Hanna laughed knowingly. "It's OK. I know."

Knew what?

This was too much. I sat up, laced my fingers, and rested my palms on top of my head with a sigh. They didn't stay there. The energy in me had evaporated. My arms dropped back to my lap.

Conall put his hand over mine. It was extra warm, and I wondered if the metamorphosis had heightened his metabolism. "If I'm here as a friend, Betony won't behave the way she does when it's just you and her."

I snorted. "You're not kidding. Have you seen the way she looks at you?"

Conall blinked in surprise. "What?"

"Never mind," I said with an eye roll, waving my hand dismissively. He had no idea the effects his looks had on females around him. The levity that Conall's presence had added to the room faded as the gravity of the situation hit me in another wave. I slumped back against the cupboards again. "LaDonna, what should I do?"

My high priestess let out a soft laugh. "You've learned by now I can't tell you how to direct your path. What I will say is what I have been thinking. If you continue to teach and watch Betony, you will have a much better idea of what she is capable of, and if she's the one you need to be concerned with. Watch the other high school students who enter your shop as well—feel them out, test their energies. It's OK to pry right now; we need to find some answers. Meanwhile, I want you also to watch yourself, monitor how the world looks through new eyes. You have seen yourself as a chaos witch for years. I'd like you to see if you notice a change in yourself now there is the possibility you may be a..."

A what? A freaking rainbow witch?

"A Summate."

"A *what?*"

Even Conall, the most well-read of us, appeared impressed by the title alone. "What is that? I've never heard of it."

LaDonna sipped her Prosecco. "They've only existed in theory before," she admitted. "There are stories in books, but nothing is known for certain about them. A witch who has the qualities of all the others. A sum of all of a witch's potential abilities."

I scoffed. "Shit. There's no way that's me."

LaDonna made that unusual flat-lipped face again, which told me she held back what she wanted to say. What she finally said was, "Murphy, I wouldn't be so sure."

Chapter 10

How to answer all Betony's probing questions without letting on that we suspected her of being a gray? I'm a horrible liar. I never bothered to learn poker—there would have been no point. The way I averted my eyes, and how the corners of my mouth pressed, the way my eyebrows and forehead rose and fell—all of them traitors to my emotions. The only aspect I had working for me was Betony's confidence that she was right about damn near every subject. She considered me to be her teacher, her guide, the gray witch, and she was the student who believed herself to be a future shadow witch. She wasn't. I hadn't pinpointed her category yet, but shadow work demanded ample introspection, which Betony avoided.

If she was a chaos witch, I could help her get a grip on her power and the mayhem that followed her everywhere. If we were both chaos witches, well, Lord help the town of Gryphon. For that matter, the rest of the county. Maybe the whole freaking world.

Hanna had brought two dog bowls and a mat—for appearance's sake—and she and I set them on top of some paper towels near the cash register.

"The health department's gonna love that," I sighed.

"It's only for a little while," Hanna said reassuringly. "We'll figure this out before anyone has time to question why you have a puppy in the store."

Conall let out a chuckle, "Yeah, and it's not like I won't behave my-self."

LaDonna and Hanna left with hugs and promises that we'd speak the next day, but Conall stayed behind. His logic was that if he was going to be my "dog" for a while, he should feel more at home with me. As if he didn't already spend most evenings and every other weekend crashing at my house.

I put a small bag of dog food, also provided by Hanna, on a shelf behind the counter near my sales ledger and a small stack of Betony's ankle socks I'd been meaning to give back to her. (She had a habit of kicking her boots and socks off after an afternoon chat session, and sometimes she'd leave the shop barefoot, boots in hand.) Hanna and I went through the trouble of tearing it open and dumping a small portion in the trash in my kitchen before bringing it into the shop, so it appeared to be slightly used. Standing behind the counter, I surveyed the shop. I guessed I passed as a new pet owner.

Turning to Conall and noticing, not for the first time, how his shoulders stretched his t-shirt, I asked, "What's it like? When you're Rolf?"

He shrugged and leaned against the counter. The wall of herbs in glass containers reflected the glimmer of streetlight coming through the front windows. "It's neat. I can smell things I never noticed as a human, and they're mind-blowing. Walking around on four legs was weird at first—I mean, the joints in my legs bend different. And being small..."

I laughed softly. "Not something you're used to."

"No," he admitted with a chuckle. "It's not easy going from over six feet to eighteen inches tall."

My brow furrowed. "I wonder where all of it goes? The parts of you that have to, um, disappear when you transfigure and then come back when you're you again."

He made an explosion motion with his hands, and his eyes grew wide in jest. "Magic," he whispered. I slapped his chest and laughed.

Holy cow, it was past my bedtime. So much had happened today. The robber. The kids taking a tour of my house. The Mystic Spiral. LaDonna and Hanna's visit. The clock hanging high on the wall across the shop read 11:20. I circled the counter and made it as far as the first table before I collapsed into a chair in exhaustion. Every emotional incident of the day hit me like a bus at once, and now the craziness had subsided, my energy was sapped.

"You need more prosecco," Conall observed. "Or would you prefer tea?"

"More prosecco would be great," I moaned. He made it as far as the passage to my kitchen before I hollered, "Right behind you!" and heaved myself out of the chair. I felt like I'd aged twenty years in the past two hours.

Moments later, we climbed the winding staircase to my living room with glasses in hand and flopped down onto my well-worn chairs, where we'd spent many a weekend. Surrounded by the walls of my home, which always smelled comfortingly of sandalwood incense, the tension in my shoulders eased a tad. It was late, and I had to open the shop in the morning, but despite my fatigue, my mind was reeling, and there was no way I was sleeping soon. I hoped the wine would help me relax enough to catch a few zz's before unlocking the door in the morning.

"Tell me about Betony," Conall coaxed. "All I know is that you've been answering her millions of questions and that she comes into the store a lot. She sure has taken a huge shine to you, especially recently."

He perched on the edge of my couch and leaned in with his glass. I watched the bubbles float to the top of the sparkling drink, and my eyes then fell to the buttons of his gray shirt. Funny. He was an orange witch but leaned toward more subtle colors: gray, light blues, subtle browns. I was a gray witch but liked bold colors—red, emerald green, deep purples.

Was I a gray witch? Or was I a—what was the word LaDonna used? A summit? Or was it summate? Fuck. I didn't know how to spell it. The way LaDonna pronounced it sounded more like an 'a' than an 'i.' For all I knew, it was an 'e.'

"Murphy?"

I blinked. Crap. He probably thought I was staring at his chest. Which, to be fair, I was. A little.

"Betony. Right. Sorry. She's... unpredictable. She's emotional."

"What sign is she?"

"Scorpio," I said. He sucked air in with pursed lips. "Yeah. Lots of potential for anger and jealousy and potent emotions there."

"Anger?" he scoffed. "Try rage."

"You're right. Rage. Her moods are all over the chart. Her home life hasn't been the best. Dad's a deadbeat who uses drugs. Mom has a history of stripping in some shady places and scraping by doing various odd jobs to pay the bills."

"Has her life always been a mess or...?"

I paused. "Has it always been chaotic? Yes, as far as I know. Or at least she paints it that way. I always thought she was painting the story a little broadly, but now..."

"Scorpios may have issues sometimes, but they tend to be honest," Conall noted.

"True," I admitted. "I'm not sure about Betony, though. She's pretty sketchy."

"Do you think she has a rising Gemini or Cancer?"

"Hey!" I exclaimed. My sun sign was Cancer, and I was the epitome of an example: old-fashioned, emotional, driven by a need for security, protective, and fiercely loyal. Not to mention a die-hard romantic.

Conall held up a palm in defense, and I noticed, not for the first time, that his lifeline was deep and long, his nails well-trimmed. "I'm sorry, but you know you Cancers can shift your conversation sideways whenever you want."

I nodded. "A rising Gemini would explain her erratic behavior. Conall, when I say she is chaotic, I mean she'll be in love with one person in the morning and head-over-heels with someone else by nightfall. I have the texts to prove it."

He breathed out. "She sounds like a handful. Why did you take her on?"

I swallowed a sip of sweet, bubbly prosecco before answering. "I never did—not formally, anyway. She started asking all these questions, and soon she was wearing a pentacle necklace, Googling about witchcraft while she and her friends hung out in the store, and asking a lot more questions. I figured better to guide her than to let her learn spells incorrectly and wind up hurting herself or someone else."

He nodded, agreeing. "True. Have you ever tried to discourage her?"

It was my turn to scoff. "There's no discouraging Betony."

He sat back and took a long sip from his glass. "Well, I can help. If I detect anything in her future when I am near her, I'll relay it to you. You can play it off as a premonition. She'd believe that, right?"

I rubbed my forehead with my free hand and tousled my hair. "Conall, what if she's a chaos witch?"

"You'll teach her to protect herself and everyone around her."

I imagined trying to tell Betony, the mother hen, the social hub of the gaggle of teens who came to the shop, that she'd need to live a life of solitude surrounded by protection spells. Betony, who snuck out of her parents' house. Who lied about where she was going to her parents. Who hedged the truth when telling stories or embellished them to the point they didn't resemble real life. Who snuck cigarettes, vapes, alcohol, and pot whenever she had the chance.

Yeah, that wasn't happening.

Now, LaDonna thought I might not be a gray, but might be a weird rainbow witch who can do whatever? I mean yeah, inside the shop, I dabbled in spells of all sorts, but that didn't make me weird, did it? It seemed to me it meant my skill set was as erratic and unsure as every other part of my life. That my single strongest skill hadn't manifested only meant the gray in me made that chaotic, too.

I wasn't the "summit" of anything, only a chaotic life that seemed to be getting worse than ever.

Chapter 11

Most Saturdays are slow but steady in the shop, and today was no exception. Conall had come back before lunch, and now "Rolf" lounged around the shop and enjoyed the "oohs" and "aahs" of the customers with plenty of ear scratches and belly rubs. Around noon, I put together an enormous ham and cheese sandwich with lettuce and tomatoes and fed half of it to doggy Conall under the counter.

My phone *pinged*, and I picked it up. It was the group chat I had gotten looped into with Betony's after-school crowd. Normally, the chat consisted of memes and selfies with the occasional banter or short video. Harmless stuff. This time, it was a text from Betony.

Bet: *Are you OK? You didn't get into trouble with your priestess, did you?*

I laughed a little. She made it sound as if LaDonna would ground me if she caught me misbehaving. Conall/Rolf's head tilted in curiosity, and I found my grin getting wider.

"It's Betony," I told him. "She asked if I got into trouble with La-Donna."

The puppy huffed and laid down, his chin on his oversized paws.

I ignored the message. The moving conversation bubble told her I'd received it, but there was no reason to jump to a response. First, I was working, and though the shop was slow, it was not my style to keep myself occupied on my phone while the store was open. Second, I still hadn't decided how to handle the whole Betony debacle of finding out if she was the gray while trying at the same time to work out if I was the Summate.

I set the phone back on the counter, face down, when it *pinged* again. Slightly miffed, I flipped it over. Lorina's red- and black-framed face popped into the profile pic next to the text bubble.

Two-tone siren song: *Mama Murph, you OK?*

One kid worrying wasn't much to concern myself with, especially if that person was Betony. She might have been digging for conversation or wanting to pry. Lorina, though, was genuinely concerned.

I'm fine. Just working.

Two thumbs-up emojis followed. I set the phone back down as

Hanna breezed through the door with a huge silver tray of muffins. The fragrance of orange and cranberry filled the coffee shop, and even though I'd finished the better part of an enormous sandwich only moments ago, my mouth watered. Hanna's muffins had that effect.

She plopped the tray down on the counter and leaned over, cooing at Rolf.

"Well, aren't you the cutest little thing?" she said as if she hadn't brought him to my house only hours before. Conall rolled over onto his back, exposing his belly. Hanna obliged him with a rub.

"Now you need to wash your hands before you put the muffins away," I scolded. Hanna gave me a grin, and Rolf's brown eyes rolled as she blew through the door to the kitchen, leaving me to put the muffins away. I set a few in a covered glass cake dish on the counter to lure customers.

The shop door opened again, and Jake and Cadence entered. I had to check my watch—it was only ten minutes past eleven. It was unheard of to see them at this hour on a Saturday. Then I realized they were on break from band and color guard. (They made the cutest couple during football games.)

"You still have the dog!" Jake exclaimed, rushing through the tables to pet Rolf enthusiastically. Cadence joined him, and they placed their orders and took a seat near the register.

Hanna blew by with a hug and a kiss and another pat on Rolf's head, quickly recording her inventory in the store register before dashing out the door to her date. A young man in a pickup truck waited for her at the curb with a broad grin on a tanned face topped with a baseball cap. Apparently, they were driving some ridiculous distance to go apple picking today. There was no end to the feats Hanna could convince men to do for her. On the plus side, the next batch of pastries would have fresh apples in them.

From the way they lingered at the counter after paying for their order, Jake and Cadence hadn't come to Witch's Brew solely for the food. When I handed them their order, they took their table reluctantly. As they ate a couple of Hanna's pastries and sipped on coffee and juice, they leaned across the small table so close their foreheads were less than a handsbreadth away. Their conversation was steady but stealthy—I couldn't make any of it out, though they sat less than 10 feet away.

After a few moments, they came to a begrudging agreement and stood so they could approach the counter together. Cadence's hand was engulfed in Jake's sturdy fingers.

"How's practice going?" I asked, as if I hadn't noticed their intense conversation that had ended only moments ago.

"Fine," Cadence replied. "My phone is blowing up today, though. Has Betony said anything to you?"

"She asked me how I was doing today and about if I'd gotten in trouble with LaDonna. That's all."

They paused together, and Jake broke the silence. "She and Amber broke up."

Again? "I hadn't realized they were back together."

"This time was bad," Cadence said with a grimace. "They got into a huge fight. Amber said she was in love with someone else and had been the whole time."

"She used Betony, and now Betony knows it."

"She's super pissed," Cadence added.

"I'm sorry to hear that," I said, keeping an eye on a customer browsing at the shelf closest to the register. The shopper had nothing in her hands yet, but I was more concerned with taking care of my clientele than the most recent high school gossip. Especially since Betony would undoubtedly have another love interest lined up by nightfall if she didn't have one now.

On the other hand, a pissed-off chaos witch could mean serious trouble. And while Betony had a history of carrying a torch for multiple people at a time, she loved them all, of course. Or so she said.

"Why are you telling me?" I asked.

From the way Jake refused to face me and took an interest in the woman browsing nearby, he didn't want to say. Cadence plowed ahead.

"We think she might do something... to get back at her."

"What? Like a hex?"

Their heads bobbed in unison. "That's why she was asking you about curses yesterday," Cadence added. "She knew it was coming and was already planning a way to get revenge."

"I can't help her with that. Well, I could, but I won't."

"Not on purpose," Cadence replied. "That was why we wanted to tell you. If she starts asking questions about stuff like that, we knew you'd want to know why."

"I appreciate it, y'all," I said.

The woman who'd been hovering nearby had made a selection from the candle display and approached the counter, hanging back so as not to interfere. I reached forward and took the candles and brass bell from her hands and smiled at her and the kids in turn, telling them with my body language the conversation was over for now.

"Have fun at practice. And thanks for the heads-up," I said, meaning it.

Their job done, Jake and Cadence began clearing the table, preparing to take the rest of their snacks with them. The woman at the counter eyed them, then me, and shook her head with a smile.

"Teenagers," she said fondly. "They seem like nice kids."

"They are," I agreed. *It's their friend I'm not so sure about.*

Chapter 12

My phone began sending me alerts by noon, but I didn't need a phone to tell me what my senses had already picked up: wonky barometric pressure and the smell of rain hanging heavily in the humid air. An unexpected storm was going to hit before nightfall, and from the way the temperature had risen and was predicted to drop, it could be a bad one.

Clouds rolled in around two o'clock, right as the traffic from the high school increased. Practice must have let out early so the kids would be safely home before the rain hit. The crowd in Witch's Brew dwindled to nothing, and I dug out the sign to hang on the door in a few minutes when I closed the shop early due to weather. It wouldn't be the first time I'd have to close because of the threat of twisters. This storm was bound to produce some rainwater that would become powerful moon water with that night's full lunar display, and this would be an excellent time to put a catch jar in my backyard.

I quickly left my perch behind the counter and strode through the swinging doors to the kitchen, where I found Conall pulling a dark gray t-shirt over his head. I tried—but failed—to tear my eyes away from his narrow waist before his dark head popped through the collar. He gave his head an extra shake to encourage his hair to fall back into place. I took the opportunity to regain my momentum and move to the island in the center of the kitchen, where I kept empty jars and a wide-mouth funnel.

"Good idea," he observed, combing his hair into place with his fingers. "Got an extra jar I can borrow? And another funnel?"

"I do. Here." I handed him a jar and the plastic funnel I'd planned on using. I headed to a cabinet in the farthest corner of the kitchen and withdrew an old metal funnel from the shelf. The texture was a strange mix of smooth with a hint of rough that brought back a world of memories. Conall chuckled.

"Where'd you get that one? A tin man in the woods? It's like the dude from Oz's hat."

I bit back the defensive response that sprang to my lips. "It was my mother's."

His cheeks colored. "I bet it has extra power in it, then," he said. His brown eyes full of remorse were all the apology I needed.

I grabbed my bag of salt and we swiftly made our way to the compass stamped into my backyard concrete—a landscaping idea I'd stolen from LaDonna. Pending storm energy charged the humid air and my skin tingled. I hastily swept a broom across the concrete, symbolically cleansing the space for the next step. Conall waited for me in the center of the circle, watching me with an amused grin. I set the bag between our feet and we faced each other with a familiar smile, him facing south, me facing north. Holy Horned God, he was cute.

Some rituals are traditions passed on for generations. Some rituals, like the one we were about to do, began among friends who used the power that sparked between them. It'd have to be a quick one so I could get back to my unattended store, but with the threat of bad weather I wasn't too worried.

Together, we raised our joined hands skyward and dropped them in a circle to our sides the way we'd done dozens of times before for various ritual purposes. Some things never change. His warm palms and thick fingers made mine look small.

I started to speak, and Conall joined me.

"God and goddess, gather 'round, come forth and bless this sacred ground."

I turned, grabbed the bag of salt and started sprinkling in a clockwise direction.

"Bless the power that enters here, formed within our sacred sphere."

Starting from the north, I sprinkled, casting a circle. Conall set our mason jars and funnels in the center before stepping outside the ring so when I joined the two ends together, the energy would remain inside until I broke it later. A fat drop of rain landed on my arm, making a cool half-sphere on my skin.

"With love, and peace, and unity. As we will, so mote it be."

I linked the ends of the circle with a smile. Casting always made me feel a little high. Casting before a storm made me positively giddy. Another fat drop landed on the top of my head, and I giggled before racing to the shelter of the back porch, Conall following like a shadow. We turned to look at our circle and jars as if we half expected the results to be immediate.

"LaDonna must have shown you how to change back to being a human without having to say anything aloud," I commented, and he nodded. We headed back into the rear of the shop together as the single droplets gained momentum, pattering on the roof of the porch.

"She made the spell so I could do and undo it alone, even though I'm not a green. It gets claustrophobic in that little body after a while," he admitted. "And she knew there was a chance I'd need to resume my human form when there would be no one to release me from the dog."

"Smart."

The bells on the shop door jingled, and I peered through the gap in the door, a little surprised to get a customer right before a torrential downpour. Damn, and I still needed to bring everything from my veranda and porches into my garage.

It was Betony, moving slowly through the tables as if she'd never stepped inside before—or saw it with new eyes. I motioned to Conall to stay back as subtly as I could and called into the shop. "Hey, Bet. You sure you want to be here right now? It's about to really come down."

Lorina followed her in with a short umbrella dripping in her hand, shooting me an apologetic glance over Betony's shoulder so her friend couldn't see. Betony had made up her red-ringed eyes with elaborate eye shadow and tiny stars at the corners in an attempt to cover it.

"Jake and Cadence might be coming, too," Betony said as if she hadn't heard me.

Conall, once again in the shape of Rolf, brushed my calves and raced out to greet the kids. Dang, he was getting fast at that shape-shifting thing. I followed him until I reached my usual post behind the counter when the store was slow.

"But the storm—"

"My mom is at work," Betony said.

Lorina shrugged. "I told my folks you had a shelter."

"Lorina!"

She chuckled. "It's not a lie. Your house is warded as hell. You don't get more sheltered than that."

While I appreciated Lorina's respect of my coven's spellcasting skills, my old Victorian would likely collapse under the fury of an F-4 tornado, should one arise, regardless of the number of incantations cast in its defense.

"I thought we could use that Spiral again," Betony said. "Lorina said she thinks her Gramma Emerson might be trying to talk to her."

Her words rang false, and I had a suspicion I knew why. Betony's grandmother was the one person who had accepted her for her whimsical, mercurial, colorful self, and Betony adored her. She had passed away almost two years ago. She probably thought if Lorina's grandmother came through again, she stood a chance to speak to her own grandmother as well. I couldn't blame her for her hope.

"Sure, we can do that," I said, "but y'all have to leave when I close. I'm planning to lock up in fifteen minutes." I pulled the board from under the counter where I'd stashed it the night before.

"In your study?" Betony asked, a hint of suppressed eagerness in her voice.

Why would she want to use my study? "No, we'll do it down here. The store is still open, and my study is for my private rituals only."

Betony didn't pout outwardly, but her arms crossed as she turned away from me and took a seat at the table across from Lorina.

Jake and Cadence came in covered in a sprinkling of rain as we set the planchette on the board. With Jake and Cadence present, we needed added table space. We pulled the same two tables together as the night before, and they circled the table to grab seats, saying quick hellos in greeting. I didn't bother to ask how they'd managed to convince their parents that it was a good idea to come here while the weather turned south. I wasn't sure I wanted to know.

I placed myself at a position that could be construed as the head, with pairs of teens on either side of the table, the board centered among them. Once again, I lit a stick of incense as "Rolf" took a seat at my feet with a long-suffering sigh.

Lorina, obviously nervous, wiped her hands on her black jeans and leaned in, extending an arm.

"Nervous?" I asked. Her hand hovered above the planchette.

"A little," she confessed.

I reached a hand forward and placed it on her arm. My fingers nearly wrapped around her entire forearm. "Don't be," I said. "I'm here, and you're inside the shop, protected. And if it's your grandmother, you'll know."

Before I let her arm go, I took a fraction of a second to tap into the Source and send a small current of energy her way. Nothing suspicious, only enough that she would likely credit her sudden self-assurance to the surety lent to her by my ten-second pep talk.

Leaning forward, Lorina placed her hand on the planchette, and I immediately became aware of a presence outside with a powerful need to enter. No name came to me, but I got a vision of them: dark, wavy hair, spindly frame, high cheekbones. From the likeness to the young woman at the table in front of me, there was no doubt in my mind it was Lorina's grandmother. I didn't say anything yet, since it could be me picking up on Lorina's thoughts channeled through the glass tool.

I hadn't used my focus or tapped into the Source when we used the board before—it had only been an exercise, and I'd been there for supervision, not guidance. We'd been inside the walls of Witch's Brew, my safe haven. This time, however, the memory of LaDonna's words echoed in my mind. Could Betony be a chaos witch and not be aware of it?

I pulled in a level of power that I usually only recruited while in the safety of my study. I made a measured effort to keep my expression void as the power surged into me, raising goosebumps on my flesh and turning the world into more than three dimensions. Every item in my presence became almost alive, energy humming through and around it. Depth and space became intuitive; I sensed precisely how my body related in space and time to every item in the room. I looked up at the kids around the table and saw the surrounding energy, and it was a wonder to me that they didn't see mine.

My aura turned to indigo with hints of silver with my connection to the Source. Witch type does not decide aura colors, and I always loved the blend of hues that covered my skin when I tapped into the Source. I peered down the table, and my eyes grew wide. Holy crap, Jake was strong. Even from where I sat several feet away, I could see red, orange, gold, and yellow colors radiating from him like solar flares. I hesitated to appreciate the beauty of it before Betony leaned forward to touch the planchette.

The moment she did, her aura, which moments before shone with a vibrant blend of reds and pinks, suddenly devolved into a riot of reds, blacks, browns, and sulfurous yellow. I clenched my teeth together and forced myself to hold on to the Source because my first impulse was to let go of the ugly sight.

"There is definitely someone here—I can feel it," she said confidently. "Gramma Emerson?"

It's not her grandmother, I thought defensively. *But she's really hoping it is. And what the hell happened to her aura?*

She was right about one thing; the moment she touched the planchette, a door opened to someplace. If not for the wards, the building would be aglow with myriad spiritual entities. I turned to the windows and eyed each one warily, half expecting to see the spectral forces swimming by the windows.

Conall/Rolf let out a light whine and rested his head on my shoe.

When he did, the warm, soothing sensation of the Source flowed between the two of us. Peeking down, the aura around him glowed brighter than that of an average dog, but my friend displayed his frequent tones of turquoise, aquamarine, and light blue. Reassured by his presence, I bowed toward the table to better see the board.

"Lorina, what are you feeling? Anything?"

Lorina shook her head, her eyes glassy. Clearly, she'd hoped to reach her grandmother this afternoon.

"Do we have to do anything to let them in?" Cadence asked. "The spirits, I mean."

"She didn't yesterday," Betony responded with a shrug.

"I did allow positive energies in yesterday. Never, ever use a board without protecting yourself first. They can't come in until I invite them," I said, looking past Betony to where Cadence sat to her left.

"You didn't do that already?"

"I was testing the barriers," I said. "A lot has been happening lately, and I wanted to make sure that any passages they used were ones I gave them."

"What if they weren't?" Jake asked.

I shrugged. "I'd cast them out."

He drew back, astonished at my blasé tone. "What if there were a bunch of them?"

"I'd be surprised," I said. "Y'all are new at this. Unless you have someone who's dying to haunt you or reach you, the barriers should be fine." It was all I could do to preserve my façade of nonchalance. The energy Jake handled and the frenzied multicolor aura around Betony worried me; I'd never seen anything like either one. I wondered if the force behind Betony's frenzied aura might have the strength to allow spirits in that did not belong.

"Can you open the door?" Lorina asked, her eyes still on the planchette as if willing it to move.

I nodded and closed my eyes so I could focus, but also so I could stop seeing the garish glow of Betony's jacked-up aura.

"Dark of night, and shining moon, may kindly spirits fill this room—"

"I didn't know she did this yesterday," Betony's voice said in a stage whisper.

My eyes flew open. "Betony. *Don't interrupt.* You should know better."

Immediately contrite, she shrank a little in her chair and bit her bottom lip. Her aura shrank as well, devolving into hues closer to her previous reds and pinks. "Okee."

I took a deep breath to refocus and imagined breathing out the negative energy like smoke. Then I did it again. It wasn't like me to be so riled up, and it peeved me that something so insignificant had triggered such a response. I hadn't realized my heart rate had picked up until I became aware of it decelerating. I opened my eyes and met everyone's gaze down the table.

"Nobody talk. Please."

"No," Lorina said, her brown eyes shooting daggers at Betony. "We won't."

I sat a little taller in my chair and closed my eyes again.

"Dark of night, and shining moon, may kindly spirits fill this room.

From north and east, from south and west, we call you forth, your presence blessed.

May we hear you true, and be heard in kind, leaving all harmful things behind."

I opened my eyes to find that everyone watching me, including Rolf. I smiled. Jake's mouth opened, closed, opened again.

"Yes?" I asked.

"You… you were…"

"Yes?" I prodded again.

"This is going to sound crazy."

"Just say it!" Cadence cried.

"Purple. You looked purple. Around…" his hands made a shape as if tracing the edges of my body.

"Do you still see it?" I asked. He shook his head.

"You're not crazy. That's my aura." I said with a grin, proud of the gentle giant.

He nodded, and his eyes darted to Betony, where her aura resumed the sickly hue, and away quickly. He'd noticed that as well, and it concerned him.

"We'll talk later. Let's see if we can get Lorina in touch with…"

The planchette stuttered and moved, and as it did, the presence of a specter hovering over the table, a thin hand guiding the piece, shimmered into view. Everyone else's eyes focused on the circle dancing under the ghost's power. Go… fish… go… fish…

"Julia?" I asked. The piece swerved to YES.

"Jake, you need to take over for Betony," I instructed.

"Why?" Betony complained. "I mean, wouldn't it make more sense for Lorina to come off? She said yesterday she was afraid she'd influence the answers."

I shook my head. "It doesn't matter now. It's her—I can see her—"

Lorina's large eyes grew enormous. "You can?"

I nodded. "Yes. Lorina. You look a whole lot like her, don't you?" She nodded, a weepy smile forming under her teary eyes. "And now we're sure it's her, it's best if Jake pairs with her. Their energies are a lot more conducive to this. The bond they built while making the band—it carries over."

"Wouldn't three people be better than two?" Her aura moved and twitched, the growth of the sulfury yellow revealing the irritation she tried to hide.

"Not this time."

Grudgingly, Betony removed her fingers and made room for Jake. His hand across from hers resembled a bear paw joining a spidery hand. The moment their energies channeled into the piece, I caught a scent of vanilla and hyacinths that came from Grandmother Emerson.

"Gramma?" Lorina whispered. She'd sensed it, too.

The planchette responded. *Yes.*

Enormous tears flowed down Lorina's face. "I miss you."

The piece stuttered around the board, slowly making its way.

Love… you…

"I love you, too." A huge sob escaped, and she sniffled and swallowed heavily. I motioned to Cadence to bring back the tissues I kept behind the counter, and she nodded and fetched them, placing them in front of Lorina, who ignored them. Her eyes locked on the board, and her limbs shook from fingertip to elbow.

The piece stopped moving, and the presence dispelled.

"She's gone," I said.

Lorina moved the planchette over to *Goodbye*. As soon as she did, a tidal wave of energy entered the room. I pressed my feet to the floor and measured the distance between myself and my salt and sage, ready to respond if needed. Without warning, the planchette jerked across the board in a broad arch.

"Stop moving it!" Lorina said to Jake in alarm.

"I'm not!" Jake cried. "It's not me!"

I held up a hand to silence them as we watched the piece racing in fervent swirls and dips. I recognized this powerful and familial energy.

"It's reading the board trying to find letters," Betony said, but I shook my head. This pattern, this strength, was one I'd seen before. As soon as I'd put a finger on it, the smells of fog and hay and heather came to me.

"It's an ancestor of mine," I said with certainty. "Aislinn Blackwell." My last name comes from my maternal line, the ancestor's Blackwell name taken from the black well behind her home in Ireland, where she, as a purple witch, foresaw the future in the water. Not for everyone, mind you; she had a select group of townspeople and visitors she trusted. Witchcraft may not be accepted in many circles nowadays, but it could get a person hanged back then.

The piece nearly flew out from underneath the fingers that held it as they swooped to a single word.

YES.

I took a deep breath. It wasn't the first time Aislinn had appeared on the circle, but it was typically with the coven. This was the first time she'd revealed herself to anyone who wasn't family.

"Mother Aislinn, what do you want to share with us?"

Wasting no time, the planchette swept to the color wheel, choosing a single hue. Looped back around again and again.

Gray… gray… gray…

"I see," I said, trying not to reveal my thoughts.

"You!" Betony crowed. "She's talking about you!"

NO… YOU… LISTEN… OTHER… CLOSE…

I sucked in a breath and asked the one question I needed an answer to.

"Mother Aislinn, the prophecy… did you mean me?"

The piece stopped moving for a moment before sliding to a single word.

NO.

My heart raced, and I fought the urge to cry as intensely as Lorina only moments ago. Not me? I wasn't cursed with chaos? Then what the hell was wrong with me? What the hell was I? Why hadn't she told me sooner? Or did she not know?

My ears rang and my hands clenched and unclenched. So many

questions had tumbled around my mind for the past two decades, and this was my first chance to speak to Mother Aislinn without the coven listening in. There was a chance she may not stay long, so I asked the most important question I needed to be answered. I didn't dare ask in English, though, so I called on some of the limited Irish Gaelic I knew and hoped I didn't mangle it too badly.

"An bhfuil sí anseo?" Is she here?

YES.

Any doubt I'd had that it was Betony vanished.

"Thank you, *seanmháthair.*"

It made one more circle before landing on *LOVE*. A ghostly kiss of air brushed my cheek and hair, and she was gone.

Well, shit.

Chapter 13

The silence around the table was palpable. No other entities revealed themselves once Aislinn fled, so I released my hold on the Source. In the distance, the deep rumbles of an ominous southern storm rolled—the type that often bred twisters. My nerves hummed with apprehension.

"Y'all better get home before this storm hits," I said.

"No way," Lorina said firmly, her arms crisscrossed on her narrow chest. "What in the hell was all of that about? You're in a prophecy? And what fucking language was *that?*"

I pulled in a deep breath and let it out, studying the paper bats hanging from the ceiling as I gathered my thoughts. "Apparently, I'm not in the prophesy," I responded. "For years, I thought I was the gray witch my great-great... well, an ancestor a long time ago predicted. And the language was Gaelic."

"I've never known anyone who's part of a real prophecy before," Jake said, his expression awed.

"She's not. She just said that," Betony teased. Turning to me, she added more softly, "And if you're not a gray witch, what are you?"

My first impulse was to answer her honestly. However, I was hesitant to tell her that LaDonna suspected I might be more powerful than a gray—more powerful than any of the colors individually. I'd feel compelled to tell them that we had deduced that Betony was the gray the prophesy foretold, which would lead to me unspooling a whole story, and Mother Goddess knew what tangles that would cause. I needed to mull over what I'd found out before I explained what it all meant to them.

"I am going to have to figure that out," I said. And that was honest, if skirting the truth a little. I'd never heard of a Summate before, so learning what it meant to be one would be an education. LaDonna had said it was a combination of all the types, but to what degree?

Another long, low peal of thunder rumbled overhead, but still, the rain only pattered on the veranda roof. Lorina peered under the table.

"Your dog is super chill," she said. "My dog would be hiding under the bed shaking from the thunder by now."

"Rolf" lifted his head and smiled the way that only a dog can. For a moment, the tension eased as everyone cooed over him and gave him pets and sweet words, and told him what a good boy he was. I shook my head. Conall was either eating it up or was doing an Oscar-worthy performance of an attention-loving pooch.

"Y'all really should go," I said. No sooner had the words left my mouth when the faint pattering of rain outside turned into fat, loud droplets. It wasn't falling with gusto now, but it would swell to a gusher within minutes. "If you leave now, you should be home before it gets bad."

"I am safer here," said Betony, which was true. Her family lived in a mobile home, which was useless when faced with the mildest of tornadoes. The urge to protect her and offer her shelter was strong, but there was so much weighing on my mind I needed to sort out.

"You can come with me to my grandfather's house," Cadence offered. "He has a shelter in his garage."

"Rolf" leaped in joy, and they all took it as a sign that Cadence's offer was a sign of the will of the universe. I fought the urge to give Conall an appreciative expression that only a human would understand.

After that, the gang left in surprising haste. Maybe they weren't as careless about the dangers of the storm as I'd assumed. Or perhaps the events of the night had creeped them out more than I'd suspected. When the last of them left, I locked the door, hung up my "Closed due to weather" sign, and faced Conall, still in his furry form. It was only four o'clock—three hours before the store would typically close on a Saturday—but the heavy cloud cover cloaked the world in an early dusk.

"What do you think?" I asked. He only cocked his head the way adorable dogs do, and I smiled.

"Come on," I said with a beckoning arm, and we headed through the swinging doors to my home. Well, I went through the swinging doors. Conall trotted under them. Some days, it struck me how odd it was that my commute consisted only of passing through a doorway. The passage itself was a symbol of leaving my business behind me and entering the sheltering womb of my home. Tonight was one of those nights. Between the way I'd explained the purpose of my mother's witchy kitchen last night and the furious storm gathering outside tonight, I'd come to value characteristics of my protected haven in a way I hadn't before.

Rolf headed to his pile of clothes in the corner and the air took on a mirage-like haze as he started to transform back into Conall. I turned away, not to give him privacy but to save myself from the urge to stare. He had no reservations about his body—Conall did his rites sky-clad regularly, and I often envied the privileged witches who saw him during ceremonies. I'd seen him in swimming trunks and had no doubt the rest of him was as faultlessly chiseled as the parts I'd seen. I, on the other hand, had no urge to let anyone see me outside my clothes. It wasn't that I found myself unattractive; it was more modesty. I'd never felt the moon on my skin and had never been drawn to do so.

Ducking into the refrigerator to put the door between my head and his body, I found the half-empty bottle of prosecco from last night and poured myself a glass. Out of habit, I faced Conall's direction and caught a flash of skin that ran from head to heel before I pivoted away again.

"Um... prosecco?" I asked as an embarrassing flush rose to my cheeks. Thank goodness I hadn't switched on all the lights.

"Sure."

I performed an odd balancing act of keeping Conall in my peripheral vision while pouring him a glass of wine. Take the glass from the cupboard. Face the same direction while reaching for the wine bottle. Remove the cork, and pour slowly, giving him time to finish. All the while, I tracked Conall's movements from the corner of my eye to avoid seeing him naked. Once I detected garments from roughly heel to shoulder, I took a handful of steps in his direction and handed him the glass.

"Thank you," he said, a tiny bit breathless from hastily dressing. His breath smelled like ozone and fresh air. He took the glass from my hand and downed a generous swallow. Eyeballing the tiny amount left, he shook his head. He found the bottle on the counter, discovered it was empty, and shook his head again, making his brown curls wave. He'd say he was due for a haircut, but I loved them.

"This won't do," he said toward the bottom of the empty bottle.

"You can have mine," I offered, lifting most of what I'd poured in his direction. He pushed a palm at it in refusal.

"No, no, no, I wouldn't dream of it. Do you have another bottle of wine, though?"

"Um..." I did a rapid mental inventory. "I think I have a bottle of red in the pantry—"

"That'll do!" he chirped and headed through the pantry door in search of the wine. I heard the click of the switch and saw the rhombus of light on the kitchen floor, minus the shadow of Conall's fit physique.

"Should be on the left, about... um... shoulder height?" I offered.

"Aha!" he exclaimed, trotting out of the pantry victoriously with a bottle of Chianti over his head. I had to laugh. Conall's energy always brought out the extrovert in me. It was one of the qualities I loved about him. In the store, he behaved professionally, even reservedly, but he was a downright energetic, adorable dork behind the scenes.

He headed to the sharps drawer where I kept the wine bottle opener, then to the cupboard for the red wine glasses. I loved that he knew my home as well as his own. His was a rental—small, one-bedroom, like many twenty-somethings. Hanna still lived with her father. It wasn't often that events had gone well in my chaotic life, but I had a paid-for home and business at twenty-six years old thanks to my mother's careful financial planning and life insurance. Some events in my life had worked out, but I would rather have my mother.

Conall poured two glasses of red wine and turned from the counter to find me still nursing my prosecco. Feigning being aghast, he clutched his chest with a splayed hand and pushed the new glass aggressively in my direction.

"Drink, woman! We're celebrating!" he ordered, and I laughed. Mother Goddess, I was going to have a hangover if I mixed white and red wine. Then the memory of how my life had turned upside-down less than an hour ago hit me. I chugged the prosecco like a frat boy downing tequila, or whatever it is that frat boys drink.

Conall whooped as I put the empty glass on my counter and accepted the new one of Chianti. I had the glass to my lips before I realized he had raised his own in preparation for a toast. I backed the glass away from my mouth and lifted it as he had.

"To not being a chaos witch," he said with an adorably cocky half-smile.

"Yeah, but—"

"Ah ah!" he said in reprimand, with a finger pointed in my direction. "No buts. Tonight, you realized that you are not to blame for any of the chaotic events that have unfolded in your life. That, my friend, is worth celebrating."

For some reason, his use of the term "my friend" bothered me tonight, but I didn't want to linger on it. Instead, I lifted the class and crowed, "To not being to blame for chaos!" Conall echoed the sentiment, and we clicked glasses. Our smiling eyes watched each other as we downed our first swallow of red and the sound of the summer storm gushing from the heavens hit the porch.

"Rain!" Conall yelled. His mood was positively manic. I wondered if the transformation had something to do with it. Tonight, however, I didn't care if the change made him high as a Georgia pine. I needed to shake myself out of the weird combination of funk and disbelief that I was in. I wasn't a gray, which was great, but it meant that I had reached adulthood and had no idea what I was. Unless, as LaDonna suspected, I was the Summate, which was a whole new problem.

"Our funnels!" he exclaimed. "Let's go see!"

There wasn't much to see, other than a torrential downpour filling our Mason jars, but sure. Why not? I followed Conall out to the porch where I had a set of wicker chairs and a small glass-topped table I'd salvaged from someone's curb and made usable again with a coat of spray paint and a few cheap cushions.

Sure enough, the Mason jars were rapidly loading up with the help of the torrential storm. Conall reached a long arm out past the shelter of the eaves, getting his hand wet as I downed another sip of Chianti. Maybe I was drinking too fast, maybe I was an inexperienced drinker, or maybe the weird-ass energy from tonight was throwing my body out of whack, but I was already tipsy.

He pulled his hand back and flicked me with his fingertips.

"Hey!"

He put his wet hand on my arm, and I smiled. I loved the energy that came from water, and he knew it.

"This is going to be great," he said, his hand warm and wet. "This storm is powerful. And with everything going on right now—"

"Lots of strength in the water," I agreed as the sound of tornado sirens reached us.

Like a good Alabamian, I checked the local news radar on my phone before heading for cover. The radar showed red and orange clouds to the distant west dancing in a rotating ballet; they weren't so close we needed to run.

"We need to get inside," I said with a coaxing hand to Conall's triceps. We searched the house for Rex, but he was hiding someplace impossible for us to find. It wasn't unusual for him to hide for half a day, only to turn up as if he'd emerged from another dimension. I hated not knowing where he was, but we needed to find cover soon.

"He's usually OK, isn't he?" he asked.

"Yeah. Let's head to the card space."

The "card space" was a section of the Witch's Brew between what was once the sitting room and the parlor where I displayed all the tarot and oracle cards. It's centrally located and has pocket doors we could lock, for what little good they'd do if the storm was furious enough.

We headed through the kitchen, and Conall paused to refresh our drinks, which I hadn't realized we had drained. Oops. I usually tried to pace myself better than this. The unrest over the last twenty-four hours had sent me into a tumult that made me careless, and now with the stress of the storm, the wine was going down like a panacea.

I cracked a couple of windows to hear the storm and the sirens better, wishing I had replaced my broken weather radio, and poked around a few more places, searching for Rex. No luck.

Conall handed me a topped-up glass of Chianti and held the remainder of the bottle in his other hand with his glass. I didn't care. There was no telling how long we'd have to harbor in the relative safety of the store. I snatched my phone charger from the counter, and we retreated to the card space, and not for the first time, I reprimanded myself for not having a storm shelter installed.

We ducked into the small hall, drew the pocket doors shut, and locked the brass locks with a twist. Once they were drawn, the sound of the storm grew muffled, and we were alone with our wine, the occasional boom of thunder, and the slanted shelves of merchandise. I wished I had thought to grab pillows to sit on. The rug that covered the hardwood floors would not help my butt if we had to stay for long.

I hadn't realized how breathless and excited I was until I became aware of my breath slowing. The frantic pace of rushing as we'd looked for the cat subsided, and I realized how close Conall was in that small space. He no longer smelled like ozone and fresh air brought about by the change; now he was more like himself—like masculine deodorant and sweat and wine. Although the other fragrances were more pleasant, the new smells hit me on a more primitive level. I allowed myself to appreciate the muscles in his arms, the way his shirt opened at his chest, the shape of his foot extending from his pants cuff, the length of his leg.

Stop it, you idiot. It's Conall!

"Where is the rotation now?" he asked, shaking me out of my reverie.

I blinked and pressed a few spots on my phone, messing up twice as I checked my phone. "Um… still near Moundville."

He breathed a sigh. "A little ways away. Good." He downed a generous gulp of wine and sat back, shifting until he found a relatively comfortable position against the displays. I turned and plugged my phone into the outlet hidden under a slanted shelf, finding myself more conscious of the way my stomach pooched as I sat up. I shot a glance at Conall as I sat tall and caught him watching the space where my shirt separated from the top of my jeans.

Great. He was watching me, too. I had no idea what to do with this knowledge.

This might be a good time to mention that I was, at twenty-six, still a virgin. Yes, it's unusual. But you have to realize that until this moment, I'd thought I was a chaos witch. Any entanglements I took on would impact anyone I touched on any level—much less an intimate one. And while I'd always loved Conall as a friend—which he had been since I was six—I hadn't allowed myself to appreciate him, or anyone else, as a man. I mean, I knew he was gorgeous, and intelligent, and sweet, and loyal, and had always told him that any girl—woman, now—would be lucky to have him. I just never considered that the woman could be me.

Closeted with him, however, as a not-chaos-witch, and after a couple of rapidly consumed glasses of wine, my impulses considered things differently. I guess I'd been a little aware that I had a crush on him for a few years, but having a crush on Conall was as safe as having a crush on a movie star—safe, because it could never happen. It was just *there*. Impossible, but fun to think about sometimes.

My mouth was dry, and I took another sip of Chianti. Maybe it was not the best idea to have more of the substance that lowered inhibitions while they were swiftly fading, but...

The silence between us drew out until it was awkward. We sat on opposite sides of the passage we'd cloistered ourselves in with our backs against the shelves and our legs stretched out before us. My eyes traveled to the bottom of his leg above his ankle and the masculine hair growing there. In my imagination, my hand was already touching his skin, seeing how his leg felt more solid and manly than my own. My cheeks, already flushed from the wine and the excitement of having to shelter from the coming storm, grew positively on fire.

"Murph?"

I had never wished for a feminine name, but the way Murph sounded coming from his mouth was so... friendly. No man says "Murph" in a moment of passion. Conall wouldn't, at least.

"Mmm?"

"Whatcha thinking?"

I looked away before my expression gave away what I was thinking. I pulled the first deck of cards from the display that I could get my hands on—the Sun and Moon tarot. The illustration on the box did nothing to change my train of thought. On it, inside an enormous lotus flower, a woman that was barely more than a stick figure sat astride a similarly sketched man. Behind them, a huge moon floated in the sky, exactly the way I'd pictured Conall and me in my fleeting fantasy a moment ago.

I licked my lips. "I'm not a gray," I said, grabbing the first thought that wasn't sex and running with it. "What does that mean? I'm over a decade and a half older than—"

"Shh," he said, leaning forward a little and putting a hand on my shin. "You'll figure it out."

I scoffed and motioned my head and gaze toward the world outside our snug, closeted cubby. "If we survive tonight," I said with a caustic laugh.

He gave me a small, genuine smile that showed no teeth as he met my eyes. "If we survive tonight."

God, those eyes were brown and bottomless, the dark fringe of lashes his only feminine physical trait. And the way he was studying me sent my heart fluttering. What the hell was happening? Was I doing this? Was the Universe throwing the two of us together? Part of me wanted to question it, but a more significant part of me was aching to go with it, to see what happened if I let this instinct?... Impulse?... Did I want to put a name on it? If I let it guide me, I ran the risk of losing a friend I'd had for twenty years.

Staring into Conall's eyes right then, I knew it wouldn't matter. If what I wanted to do changed our relationship, it wouldn't end it. It might evolve. Shape it in a way I hadn't expected. But Conall wasn't going to leave. What we had ran too deep for that.

His hand was still on my leg, long after he might have removed it. Had we lived through moments like this before, and I was too closed off, too wrapped up in being a calamitous gray to notice?

Well, I was noticing now. Our eyes locked, afraid to break away for fear the spell we were under might sever. It was then I knew that he wanted me, too.

Throwing the deck of cards to the floor, I rushed on my knees across the floor to Conall. He moved his hands to my arms, my face, my hair as I dove for his lips like I was drowning for them.

It was as if my body had waited for this moment to recognize what physical love was. My previous experiences with sexual affection had always been short-lived and disappointing—botched kisses, unfulfilling touches, regrettable tries at a connection I knew could never last. Not this.

My hands instinctively roamed his body, and it was as though he had the same inherent knowledge of mine. There was no time for gentleness. Everything about our movements was intense, passionate, greedy, pressing. My lips crushed his as he lifted my hips and set me astride him, forcing my body against his with strong hands. Our hips moved in a tempo that I'd never experienced, had only seen in movies, but now made perfect sense. In less than a minute, my adrenaline spiked, and my breath was rushed, punctuated with kisses.

Our eyes were transfixed as he pulled on my shirt, wanting to lift it over my head. I cooperated, my hands scooping the hem of his as well and lifting it, signaling my need for his flesh. Shirts shed, the texture of his bare skin against mine left me gasping. His body was as beautiful as a sculpture. Had I experienced anything so intimate before? So perfect? It wasn't enough. I moved for the fastener of his pants.

The potential danger of the storm was completely forgotten as we shrugged out of our clothes. The sight of him naked—which I'd avoided minutes before—exhilarated me. The way his broad shoulders tapered to his waist—the strength of his body. I ran my fingers over the "As above, so below" tattoo on his left bicep. I'd been there when he'd had that set into his flesh. I'd never dreamed I'd caress it under my fingertips, kiss it with such desire.

I started to recline, pulling him with me, and Conall hastily put some of our shed clothing underneath so I wouldn't be bare on the worn rug. I lay back, and he positioned himself above me, his arm and abdominal muscles standing out with the effort. God, he was beautiful. He kissed my face and neck fervently. I reached down, found him, and began maneuvering him inside of me. He paused.

"Are you sure?" he asked, breathless and flushed as well. Strong. Caring. Concerned. He knew he would be my first. I had no secrets with him.

I nodded, and he nodded as well, lowering himself to give me one final breathtaking kiss before he pushed inside.

My body, brimming with emotion, came more alive than I knew was possible. The feel of him around me, breathing the air he breathed as he moved inside me, made me feel cherished, beautiful. The world could have fallen apart, my house blown into slivers around me, and I don't think I would have noticed anything but Conall and that moment. I was no stranger to self-stimulation, but having a man I cared for touching, caressing, and kissing me as I experienced arousal—I had no idea until now how exquisite it felt.

Conall's movements became stronger, more urgent as his arousal grew. A light sweat formed on his brow as he moved, covered my fingertips as I moved my fingers through the waves in his hair. I loved the way he watched me with need as he moved, loved my body's response as my hips rose to meet his.

I don't know why I felt driven to do it; I didn't think anything on earth could make this moment better. I suppose some part of me wanted to experience the spiritual side of our joining as well. I reached for the Source and let it in.

Conall and I both gasped as the power coursed through me and into him. Barely aware of the ground beneath, becoming one spirit with him, it was as if we were levitating. The lights inside the closet died, a victim of the storm, but I didn't need to see to feel. Blood roared in my ears, and pressure grew in my ears as I gripped his back. He convulsed with one final, powerful push that triggered a climax of my own. I cried out loudly—there was no holding it back. I'd had orgasms before, but nothing like this. I'd felt the Source before, but never like this. I had kept separation—a sense of where I drew a line between Source power and my spirit. With Conall, that need for control was shattered, and with it came openness to the power and mysteries that I'd always kept at arm's length.

Conall collapsed to my side and pulled me against him, pressing my body to his as we lay together on the pile of clothes we'd shed. Our auras blended into a beautiful mixture of aquamarine and indigo that played and tumbled around each other, caressing and flowing and blending and coming apart again. I understood the Beltane rite a lot better now—the reenactment of the goddess and the god joining. I felt like that goddess. I felt like every goddess.

"God, Murphy," he gasped, his voice thick with lust. "Holy fucking god and goddess."

I was wrong. Conall would say my name in a moment of passion.

And damned if it didn't sound beautiful.

Chapter 14

The world crept back into focus, the reality of life outside of our closeted shelter clearer once I released the Source. It felt like cutting off my heartbeat and left me short of breath. I'd never sensed the loss of that power so tangibly before.

"You OK?" Conall asked, lowering his head slightly, so his face was level with mine as he held my hand. I wasn't sure if he meant because we'd just had sex, or because I'd had to release the deluge of the Source that had been channeling through both of us until then. The answer was the same either way. I nodded. He did, too.

"Good." We lay together, my head on his arm facing him, our legs intertwined, for a few moments while we caught our breath. He played with the way our hands wove together, fingers interlaced, stretched, and clasped again. When the floor started feeling hard under our backs, he gathered his clothes and got as far as pulling on his boxers before pausing. I stopped collecting my clothes together to see why he'd paused.

"Have you ever—" he cut himself off, obviously wanting to complete his thought but wary of my reaction.

"Yes?"

He tugged his jeans up to his hips, then stood on his knees to fix the fastener before continuing. "Have you ever wanted to say something, but you were afraid to say it, because you knew if you did, it would change everything?"

I'd managed to tug my brassiere halfway on before his words registered, and I didn't mean to freeze, but I did.

He hastily crossed the small distance to me on all fours, his face managing to be fearful and earnest and pleading all at once. I drew my bra into place and snapped the clasp behind me, wishing this hadn't gotten uncomfortably emotional so quickly. He lifted a hand and rested it on my forearm, his eyes boring into mine.

"I love you, Murphy Blackwell."

Holy shit. A part of me was doing cartwheels and setting off fireworks. Part of me was scared to death. And yet another part was confused as fuck. My mouth opened, but nothing came out. It was as if the one hundred thoughts that came to mind became stuck between my mind and my voice box.

Conall quickly followed up with, "You don't have to say anything now. I don't expect you to. You've had a lot thrown at you in the past day or so, and I know you have a lot to process and unpack. But I wanted you to know—especially after—" he motioned to where we'd had sex, "I love you. I've loved you for as long as I can remember. And if after tonight, you don't think you feel the same way, please know that this was so special to me. That I've wanted this. God, I've wanted this."

He had? How had I not noticed before? Was I so closed off, so blind?

"Conall, I—" I what? I loved him, too? I mean, I did, but I didn't know how exactly to express the thoughts tumbling through my mind. I adored him. I cherished his friendship. I thought he was one of the two most beautiful human beings in my life, Hanna being the other. And he was breathtakingly handsome. The thought of my life without him was heart-wrenching. Was this what love was? True love?

"Thank you. You know… you know I adore you. So fucking much." I put a hand alongside his jaw, where the dark line of his beard grew, and my fingertips caressed the beginnings of stubble. God, I wanted to kiss him, to lay back down and have him naked and sweating over me again, wanted to curl up in his strong arms and say so much more. I longed to say it back, but I loved him too much to say it back—to say it like *that*. "I just need to… yeah, process is the right word."

He nodded and put a hand on top of mine, leaning his face into my palm. He came across as if he was struggling to be brave and put on a face satisfied with my answer. I wanted to give him more. When I considered a life without another night like tonight with him, my heart ached. I wanted more. A lot more. I held that thought back.

Process. Yes, take the time to handle it all first. Come back to this when you've thought about it more.

I didn't want to pull my hand away, but I became acutely aware of my semi-nakedness and slowly disentangled our hands. We finished dressing in silence, and I put the tarot deck back on the shelf.

"Do you hear the siren?" he asked. I shook my head.

"I haven't heard them for a while now," I admitted, leaving out the part that I didn't think I'd have noticed anything outside the small space that had made up my whole life for the last half an hour.

When Conall stood and slid the doors to our makeshift shelter open, I heard a light patter of rain. The siren had stopped.

"We survived," he said, offering his hand to help me up. Together, we grabbed our glasses and the bottle of Chianti and headed back to the porch. When I stepped outside, humidity hit me so hard a sheen of sweat instantly coated my skin. The smell of rainwater lingered in the air, but it was the sight that greeted us that left me gobsmacked. As far as I could see down Oberon Street, trees and downed power lines tilted at severe angles. The twister had torn the roof off the house across the street and removed chunks from the houses on either side of mine. Wooden fences from all the surrounding homes lay flat on the ground. As far as I could see, roof shingles, insulation, branches, leaves, and other debris littered the streets and yards. Someone's mailbox lay in the center of the road with a wide dent in its center. A little further down, I saw the tangled mess of what had once been a trampoline. A metal shed behind my neighbor's house was nearly unrecognizable.

"Conall! Oh, Mother Goddess!" I dashed inside the darkened storage room for a flashlight, then out to the yard so I could survey the damage to my home and everything around it. In my shock about my great ancestor's revelation and the whole thing that followed with Conall, I hadn't put any of my outside furniture or plants up. Everything had probably blown clear down the street.

I reached the street, noting as I did the sinister low-hanging clouds over our heads had broken up to reveal a surprising number of stars in the holes between them. Conall followed, his body as tensed as my own. The worst had passed, but the sky still clung to a lovely ominousness. The rain had stopped, and the moon struggled to poke out from behind the clouds.

The roof of my house appeared intact from the street, and I breathed a little easier. I ran to the side with Conall at my heels, panning my house with the flashlight as I surveyed my home for damage and wishing I'd mowed my yard more recently as the wet grass slapped against my jeans. Conall had switched his phone flashlight on and was inspecting as well. My siding was fine. Roof intact, as far as I could tell. No shingles appeared missing.

I panned the flashlight up and down every section as I ran, and the more I surveyed, the more none of it made sense. My yard décor hadn't budged. My wind chimes, unlike James Bond's signature martini, were stirred, not shaken. My plastic planters hadn't toppled. My wicker furniture hadn't moved.

The surrounding homes didn't just have damage—they were dirty, the siding and bricks peppered with mud and specks of flying debris. Not on my house. If anything, the rain had made it cleaner.

I reached for Conall's arm and gripped it fiercely. "Conall…"

He swallowed, his expression as astonished as I imagine mine was.

We kept walking, kept examining, kept our flashlights moving like spotlights across the siding, but the further we went, the more our assumption was proven true. "Your house wasn't touched," he breathed.

From the backyard, I saw the neighbors on Titania Street behind me were also missing most of their roof and their upper story. My breath caught in my throat as I saw the family who lived there surveying the damage. One woman clenched a hand to her chest in despair. Her wife held her hand tightly, her free hand over her mouth as their daughter, only a toddler, held a worn bunny to her side.

I kept walking, kept searching, scanning from foundation to shingles, but saw no signs that anything but rain and a little wind had disturbed my home when I'd reached Oberon Street again.

"Did you protect your home somehow? Or the coven?"

"Nothing that would withstand a twister like this."

I thought about the surge of the Source coursing through the two of us as we lay entwined on the floor inside the card space of Witch's Brew. The pressure in my ears as we climaxed. My pulse quickened as I remembered how strongly my emotions had been running as Conall and I... had sex? Made love? Had I subconsciously protected the house with the power of the Source? Or was this merely an extension of the power of the Lughaidh?

The Lughaidh, whose protective spells hadn't kept a robber from coming in during daylight hours.

The heat around my body evaporated into the sultry air, and a chill hit hard in the post-storm breeze. Goosebumps raised, and I drew in a sharp breath. Conall drew me close and ran his hands over my arms for warmth. He smelled like sweat and sex and deodorant, and I sank into his warm embrace gratefully, resting my head on his chest as if it was perfectly natural. It's not like he'd never held me before, but tonight it stirred all new emotions.

"I don't know," I said honestly. "I really don't know.

☽○☾

I offered my neighbors a place to stay the night, but they made phone calls (thankfully, all the phone towers weren't knocked out) and found family or friends who would house them for the evening, possibly longer. That done, Conall and I headed back inside with our Mason jars of storm water and capped them. My internal radar tracked his physical presence with every step, and I found myself wondering if he watched me as I moved. As I stashed my jar inside a cabinet of magical supplies, Rex reappeared, the little bugger, winding around our ankles and meowing for the dinner he'd never received. I popped a can of his favorite food and spooned it into his bowl, grateful he was OK.

Conall leaned to pet Rex, who was downing his kitty pate, and Rex arched his back as he ate, accepting the attention the way he did with so few humans. I thought about the way he'd responded to Betony recently.

"What?" Conall asked, reading my features.

"Betony," I said. "Rex hated her."

Conall's brows arched as he considered that, his expression darkening as he watched Rex down his dinner. "You think he knows something."

"Yeah."

He stretched an arm down and stroked Rex's jet-black fur. The cat arched once before diving back into the bowl like a starving beast, the spoiled brat. "Betony's the Grey."

I nodded, a tightness in my chest as I admitted it. "Yeah. She is."

Chapter 15

In the morning, I realized that I'd been careless in not telling anyone that I had survived the storm. In the morning, the power was still out in the neighborhood, but the charge on my phone was enough to make a couple of posts on social media before the battery died. I let both my personal and professional groups know that I was OK, but Witch's Brew would be closed until power was restored—most likely for at least 24 hours.

I shuffled back outside in my worn gray slippers to survey my house in the morning sunlight. The rumble of generators, hammers, and power tools disturbed the normally quiet Sunday morning. My siding, gutters, and window boxes of herbs looked the way they would any other day, only wetter and smelling a tad greener from the rain. I couldn't be one-hundred percent sure that I wasn't missing a shingle or two without getting a better view at the roof, but I would have wagered that my house was intact.

Conall emerged from the kitchen carrying two iced coffees he'd found in the fridge, his hair tousled from sleep. God, he looked good. He strode to my side and examined the house as well. Although we'd spent the night wrapped up like snakes in the same bed, he didn't encroach on my space; he handed me a bottle with a small smile. He might have been standing a little closer than he would have two days ago, but that might have been me being more aware of him and his energy.

"Anything?" he asked as I took a sip of coffee. It was still a little cool despite spending the night in a refrigerator with no power, but I would have killed for a cup of warm brew with some cream.

"No, nothing."

He scanned the side of the house and the yard as well. We headed to the veranda and took seats across from each other at the iron bistro set. Despite the drone of generators and the periodic sound of hammering nails and sawing boards, it was a surprisingly peaceful morning.

I sipped my coffee and thought about how chaotic life had gotten in the past two days. I panned my pristine yard, my eyes settling on the neighbors, who were hammering plywood over their windows as a makeshift barrier until their windows could get repaired.

"I wish I could help," I said softly.

"You could," Conall offered. "I'm going to head to the house for my equipment after we're done with our coffee so I can drive around and see where I can lend a hand. You could join me."

I shook my head, my heart heavy with the ache to help my neighbors. "I'd better not," I said. "Not until I understand my power as a Summate, or whatever I am. Until I do, I run the risk of having 'Murphy's Law' cause more damage than good. I need to help Betony figure out her power, too. That way, I can get a handle on deflecting her gray energy."

"I've been thinking about that," he said. "The only way we're going to know if we *can* help her is to find out how she uses her chaos or if she's using it at all."

"Conall, I've heard three years of her stories. Even if she's only exaggerating a tiny bit, her whole life has been nothing *but* chaos."

"But is that her fault?" he inquired. "Is she *causing* it?"

I opened my mouth to respond but closed it when doubt set in. "I don't know. I mean, she thrives on it in a way I never have. When the chaos hit me, I just wanted to curl into a ball in bed and hide like a crab in its shell. She's not like that at all. When her life goes sideways, she has enough energy to talk to all of her friends and spread the chaos power that fuels her into them and their lives."

He put a hand to his mouth, his brow furrowed in contemplation. "What if we figured out a way to test her?"

I took a swallow of my coffee, disappointed the small bottle was already gone. Bottled coffee never lasted long enough. I capped it and set it on the glass tabletop.

"I don't know how we could do that," I said, frustrated. "We'd need to find something consistent about her and stir her up to trigger her, but she changes what she wants to do when she graduates every few months. Her friend circle outside of the kids you've met changes constantly. She changes who she says she's in love with every other day—"

He snapped his finger and pointed at me. "That might be your quickest method, then. That emotion—attraction—is incredibly powerful. Can you use that somehow?"

I considered that. It wouldn't be like using true love against her, which would be unethical. Despite what she called it, Betony's feelings ran shallower than she believed. I hoped one day she would find someone that would make her feel the way Conall had made me feel last night. And again, this morning.

Color rose in my cheeks, and I realized that my eyes were downcast, studying the paint that had started to peel on the veranda near my toes.

"Murphy?"

"Yeah—yeah, we could do that. I know Amber just broke up with her, but knowing her, she had someone on the back burner the whole time. Probably a couple of someones."

"Can you find out who?"

I scoffed. "Who she broke up with, or who she had on the back burner?"

He chuckled. "Either. Both."

It was my turn to chuckle; then, my face lit up as I sat up with excitement. "That's it!" I exclaimed. "We invite Betony to be in the same room with both the person who broke up with her *and* the person—or people—she wants to be with next. If *that* doesn't bring out her chaotic energy, I don't know what will."

Conall nodded thoughtfully. "Not a large risk of damage or death in that trial. How do you figure you can pull that off?"

"A Samhain party?" I said. "We could invite the coven over, too. They could help somehow."

Conall nodded. "That could work. The twelve of us, plus you. Betony and her friends. Do you want to have it at Witch's Brew?"

"Sure. But not until the shop closes. I won't risk a customer getting hurt."

"Of course. When do you think would work?"

I wished I had the calendar on my phone handy so I could check the dates for conflicts. "Think we can pull something together in a week? I was planning on having my usual Halloween open house at the Brew. We can have the usual open house while the store is open Saturday and then carry on with a private party after where we give Betony a test of her chaos power."

"Perfect," he said. He set his bottle on the table next to mine, and our hands touched. He started drawing his away, but I softly grasped it in mine. Our eyes met, and his dark brown eyes drew me in. My entire body felt flushed as our hands explored, first fingers, then palms. It wasn't enough. We went back inside.

☽○☾

The coven held a meeting seven days before Samhain to arrange for the holiday ceremony and festivities afterward. I seldom attended any coven meetings, ritual or otherwise, so when Hanna and I pulled her Honda into the shady driveway of LaDonna's home, an unique blend of treehouse and cathedral on the hilly side of Gryphon, apprehension set my stomach fluttering. No matter how much time I spent with my coven, I always felt like an outsider. They had never given me a reason for that—on the contrary, they always invited me to the sabbats, birthday celebrations, baby showers, and handfastings. I distanced myself from them for more than one reason. One, because I cared about them and wanted to protect them from the chaos and the damage I left in my path. But if I was honest with myself, it was also because of my natural tendencies toward introversion.

What would it be like if it wasn't me—if Betony's arrival in Gryphon hadn't affected my Summate powers? And what *were* my Summate powers?

Once again, a wave of anxiety surrounded me. I gripped the sides of the car seat, pulled in a slow breath, held it in a moment while my lungs felt like full balloons, and let it out slowly. My heart rate fell a little. The weather had remained pleasantly cool since the storm had blown through three days prior, but I perspired despite the partially rolled-down windows.

Hanna, empath that she was, took my hand in hers, which was warm, and her nails were perfect pink ovals. Her brown eyes crinkled at the corners as she smiled, but her eyes stayed large. Her teeth were as straight and white as something you'd see in a toothpaste commercial.

"You always get nervous when we come here," she scolded. It was more than that, and I'm sure she recognized my tension.

I pulled in another breath of crisp air. It smelled of pine and fallen autumnal leaves. "I know," I said. "I can't explain it." Brown and orange maple leaves tumbled by on the breeze, holding my attention. To my right, a blue late-model Camaro pulled into the spot nearest my door.

Conall.

My breath caught in my throat, and my heart, already beating fast, set off in a sprint. I still hadn't said anything to Hanna about what had happened between Conall and me, but now that we were within feet of each other, I heard her struggle to suppress a gasp.

Damn red witch power. Of course, she would know.

Her struggle to keep her face composed failed miserably. "Murphy!" she whispered between clenched teeth. "You and Conall? When?"

"During the storm," I admitted. *And several times since then.*

She was fighting her emotions now, trying not to relay too much to Conall as he got out of his car; her eyes sparkled, and her mouth turned up in a barely subdued smile. She suppressed it by pulling in her lips, making her look humorously toothless, but she gave in and burst into a wide grin again. She squeezed my hand before releasing it and opening her door.

"About damn time," she joked under her breath. "Do you have any idea how much I wanted to love spell you two, so you'd see what was in front of your damn noses? I can't believe you didn't *tell me!*"

I wanted to clap back, but she swung her door wide, exiting her car, and I didn't want to retort too loudly. Instead, I got out and stood and stretched, my thick-soled black boots silent on the paved driveway. I was glad I'd opted for comfortable jeans and a sweater tonight instead of the dressier slacks and blouse I had considered. My first impulse was to show up in a t-shirt that said "Resting Witch Face," but Hanna had talked me out of it. Instead, I'd gone with a seasonal sweater the color of fall oak leaves woven through with enough black that I could wear my favorite boots. It wasn't snug, but it did cling in a few flattering places that drew Conall's gaze.

"Hey Hanna!" he called in greeting and pulled me in for a hug. His body language was friendly toward me, but not necessarily more than a casual observer would read into; he was giving me a chance to play our interaction off as strictly friendly if I wanted to. I don't know why—unless Hanna had her back turned toward us, and her aura perception turned off, she was reading every nuance of our unspoken communication as clearly as closed captions. She didn't have her back turned toward us, though, the little heifer.

"Hi," he said, his voice low and husky in my ear. That did it. I tilted my head in a way that also allowed him a choice to change what followed—he could kiss me or just take the hug. To my relief, he took the kiss. He tasted like spearmint gum. Warmth shot from my lips to my center, and I pulled back after a moment, embarrassed because Hanna had likely sensed every one of my emotions, even the naughty ones.

"Hi," I whispered back like a giddy teenager. In my mind, we'd retreated into his car and were testing how far back the seats reclined.

"You ready?" he asked. I blinked. Oh yeah. We were here to talk about Samhain and Betony.

I pulled away from him, and the autumn cold rushed to my front where his body had been. I shrugged. "As I'll ever be."

He offered a hand, a hopeful expression below his raised eyebrows, and I regarded it for a moment. Hanna's awareness that we'd moved beyond friendship was one thing, but the coven? Then again, who was I kidding? They all had various gifts of perception. What had happened between Conall and me wouldn't remain a secret for long. And I needed his strength.

I wove my fingers through his, and the three of us headed inside.

Chapter 16

I took a moment to say hello to Hanna and Conall's fathers before we sat down. Hanna's father, Rafael, had new glasses since the last time I'd seen him. They complimented his handsome face and gray hair, and I told him so. Paul Berry looked like an older, gruffer version of his son, his hair thinner and his muscles softer with age and disuse. Despite having a face that looked grumpy and serious, Paul's face lit up easily whenever he saw Hanna and me. He gave each of us a bear hug and a kiss on the cheek, and we made pleasantries for a few minutes before taking seats across the room.

LaDonna insisted on covering the standard business first, so we spent the first few minutes of the meeting going over the Samhain ritual ceremony and the usual meal that took place after. I sat without contributing through this part, unsure whether I would participate with the coven or celebrate as a solitary practitioner the way I did most holidays. My feet wiggled in anticipation, and when Conall gave me a sideways look, I stopped and turned my fidgeting to wiggling my toes at the end of my boots.

Maybe Conall could join me, I thought, then dismissed the notion. I wouldn't want to pull him away from his father and the community of the coven so that I had someone to practice a ritual with. There had been one Samhain about five years ago when Hanna, Conall, and I had done our ceremony separate from the coven. It was done more to declare our independence than out of need. The two of them typically headed to the coven for traditional rites, where I preferred to cast my holiday circles alone. We had done several non-holiday circles on the patio behind my house, though, when spelling for good fortune, intuition, grounding, or other needs.

My brow furrowed as I considered the Beltane ritual. It was one of the few times when our coven joined with one or more local covens around Alabama, Georgia, and Mississippi, an enormous bonfire to celebrate the coming of spring. LaDonna assumed the role of the May Queen, and one male in the coven, usually her partner Luke, took the part of the Green Man who consummated the union between earth and sky. From the stories I'd heard, energy ran high that night, and it was not unheard of for there to be more than one consummation that took place that night. Had Conall ever—?

"Murphy?" LaDonna's smoky sweet voice broke through my reverie. I blinked. "Yes. Sorry?"

LaDonna smiled like an understanding mother, and I wondered if she'd somehow known what I'd been pondering. "Would you join me so we can explain to the others what you and I discussed the other day?"

I blinked. "Sure."

Rising from my seat, I moved to the head of the circle and settled myself to LaDonna's side. Together, we shared the discussion she and I had with Hanna in my kitchen a few nights before.

"If I'm correct," LaDonna concluded, resting a hand on my forearm, "Murphy isn't the Grey at all."

"I'm—I'm not," I breathed. "And I know who is."

LaDonna faced me with a bemused smile, and I continued the story, adding my ancestor Aislinn's arrival to the Mystic Spiral the other night and her clarification that I wasn't the gray, but the gray was nearby.

"It must be Betony," I said. "That would explain things."

One woman in the group, Terry, who was about LaDonna's age with waist-long, brown hair and black-rimmed glasses, spoke up. "If you aren't the gray, Murphy, that would be a little odd, wouldn't it? That you haven't found your calling?" That was a polite way of saying that something stunted me in my path, clueless about my strength.

LaDonna tilted her head to the side in acknowledgment of Terry's words and continued. "I believe that Betony's arrival in Gryphon at the age when Murphy would have been coming into her power scrambled her gift. She never came into her own because we deferred to Nora's prophecy, thinking it meant Murphy when it meant Betony instead." I loved my high priestess's confidence in my conclusion.

Joey, a sturdy, balding man with a salt-and-pepper beard, leaned in until his chest was almost over his leather boots. "What about Murphy?" I heard what his concerned voice implied. What about all the chaos that followed me? Why didn't I know what I was?

LaDonna smiled softly and turned her focus to me. "Murphy, how is your gift of prophecy?"

I shrugged. "At the shop, it's great. I can read the cards well, and I can use a pendulum to read. Or whatever's handy."

"Ever hex anyone?"

"Sure, when the occasion called for it."

"And?"

I shrugged again. "They were hexed."

"It worked?"

I scoffed before I could stop myself. "Of course."

"You've grown plants in your home, right?"

"With Hanna's help. And y'all's. You know how the plants I tried to grow at your house did."

"Ever use them? The ones at your house?"

"In spells and charm bags, sure. All the time."

"Effectively? Without killing the plants or harvesting too much?"

"Well, yeah," I said, my brow knitting. This line of questioning was confusing me. Was it odd that I had known what too much was?

"Ever lay hands on anyone in the shop to help them figure out which organs needed a certain spell or oil or—"

"Yes. LaDonna, what are you driving at?"

"You can do all of that?" Joey asked, his brown eyes stricken with amazement. He had leaned forward so far that I feared he was about to fall out of the wooden chair.

"Yes, of course. Inside the shop—"

"Inside Witch's Brew, and within the protected realm of her property's bounds, she has been shielded from Betony's chaos energy," LaDonna said. "There, she demonstrates all of her gifts without limits. Hanna, Conall, is she correct?"

My friends nodded solemnly, and I realized; I'd never seen Conall try to touch someone to find out their illness. I'd never seen Hanna try to foresee the future or perform a hex. They always stayed in their specialty, whereas I could do all the skills I'd tried my hand at, as long as I was within my protected walls. They deferred to me when those talents were required to help someone. I'd always assumed it was because it was my store, and they hadn't wanted to overstep their roles.

I'd given up on green witchery after my failed effort while living with LaDonna. Yet, when I moved into Blackwell Manor, I tried again and must have protected the plants growing inside my home from the chaos influence. The herbs I dried never molded or fell apart.

Murphy, how is your gift of prophecy?

I recalled last summer, a sultry night laying in the backyard on a blanket with Conall, staring up at the stars. He'd been stood up for a date and had come to my house afterward to talk and hang out and take his mind off it.

"You don't have anything to worry about," I said. "There's someone in your future, I'm sure of it. You're a Capricorn."

He nodded, and the back of his hand had brushed mine. I wrapped mine around his, attuning to his energy while I comforted him, and turned my attention to the sky, pointing upward.

"You're... there," I said, pointing to the nine twinkling lights that ages ago was named the sea-goat of Capricorn. "And she's..." my hand, with its extended finger, swooped in loops and dips over the heavens until it came to rest at six stars on the other side of the sky. "Over there. She's a Cancer, like me!" I didn't know why, but I knew it was right. Conall chuckled, either amused or placated. I didn't care which, so long as he was happy.

"I can try to do a deeper dive. See what I can figure out with a pendulum or—"

Conall let out another soft laugh and turned to me, his eyes soft with affection. "It's OK. I can wait."

He could wait. Even then, it was me he wanted. I swallowed a lump in my throat that hadn't been there a moment ago.

My daydream was broken when Miriam shifted her bleached-blond hair behind the shoulder of a straight-from-the-office blazer. "Are you saying she has all of those talents if she tries?"

"It's more than that," LaDonna said. "I believe she is a Summate."

Chapter 17

Over the next few minutes, LaDonna answered questions I'd been harboring since her revelation as the coven showered her with inquiries. A Summate had not one or two of the skills all witches were born with, but all of them—or at least as many as they cared to manifest. The potential was there to be any color of the spectrum or all of them at once.

All of them except gray, that is. When a gray came along roughly once every 500 years, a Summate appeared on the earth in the same generation. Sometimes they were born near one another, sometimes across the globe, but they always crossed one another's path when the universe needed a significant change. A Summate was the yin to a gray witch's yang. Calm in a storm. Light in the dark. A harbor in the storm. Choose your favorite metaphor. If Betony was, as LaDonna and I suspected, a gray, I was the spectrum of color and light to counter the shadow and balance the universe.

Or at least that's how the stories went. LaDonna and I would be doing more research into the subject to separate fact from fiction.

Since my new potential as a Summate would not be settled that night, we moved to the problem of Betony as the gray witch and how we, as a coven, could step in and help. The details were loose, but we intended them to be that way so events could flow as they needed to as they unfolded. I'd invite Betony and the others in her friend group to come to a small Samhain party with two of Betony's "love interests." The coven would be with me to see how the drama unfolded and to intervene if events turned south.

I stressed that Betony was earnest in her convictions, as confused as they might be. That she sincerely believed what she called love was real, which made her emotional state even more potent. I was glad to see heads nodding around the room in understanding. We'd all been young once; we understood the strength of teenage emotion. The power of belief, after all, was what gave the Craft its strength. Spell work without intention was useless and a waste of one's tools, breath, and energy.

Together, we talked. Contemplated. Put ideas together, added notions, and drafted timelines of theoretical results. Having a set "plan" was a surefire strategy for failure, so what we intended to do was to allow the universe to guide us as the evening unfolded. Our goal was to help Betony recognize that she is the gray and give her the guidance she needed to keep herself and those around her safe.

We dimmed the room to candlelight and a few soft lights in

LaDonna's drawing-room perimeter. In the center of the room, La-Donna and her partner, Luke, placed the enormous Lughaidh clan caul-dron filled with gathered rainwater. The thirteen of us circled it with Luke at the head. LaDonna took a small, purple canvas bag from her fireplace mantel, withdrawing black lava salt and sprinkling it around the outside of the circle. Her hands were weathered, her steps graceful and silent on the wooden floor. Her voice, deep and melodic, spoke in her preferred language for casting—Latin. She taught me that it was best to cast in whatever language made me feel the power of my words. I preferred English most of the time, but others cast in Gaelic, and one coven member fancied French. The point was to imbue the words with intent, using whatever made one feel most powerful.

When she passed behind me, I caught a few words of the spell she was casting, *"… bono malum superate…"* Overcome evil with good. It was one she used many times, and the reassuring words touched my soul like soothing music.

When she finished with the salt, she replaced the canvas bag and fol-lowed her path clockwise around the coven with her athame.

The circle was cast and the spell woven. It was time to join our ener-gies. Twelve coven members clasped hands, palm to palm, solemnly but with the natural ease that comes from familiarity. I was the last one to touch hands. It was as if part of me wanted to be sure that everyone was taking part before I added myself to the circle.

Conall was to my right, and Hanna placed herself to my left to insu-late me from any reluctance I might be feeling. I grasped Conall's hand first, finding strength and love in his firm grasp. By comparison, Hanna's hand was soft and smaller, more like my own, but her energy was no less caring. As her fingers wrapped around mine, our palms touching, it was as if a circuit completed and a channel of power opened, flowing through us all. It was similar to the Source, but it wasn't right, like an instrument tuned a half step off-key or like getting a kiss from a soulmate without passion. My heart longed for the full depth of connec-tion, the intense craving for a sensation that went beyond physical touch. It brought me back to that moment with Conall, cloistered between shelves stacked with tarot decks, protected from the storm, closeted in-side our private moment of love, of power.

I had seen LaDonna channeling the power of the Source during sab-bats, and a couple of others could use it as well. They always kept the flow they wielded to a modest drip or, in LaDonna's case, a steady but unintimidating current, like a running faucet. I frowned. This wasn't a moment to keep power in reserve. If there was a gray witch unknowingly wreaking havoc and causing heartache and damage in her path and others, we needed to help her recognize it and take responsibility for her power. I knew how headstrong Betony was. If she was the challenge we'd be facing, it wouldn't be easy.

I squeezed Hanna's and Conall's hands and tapped into the Source. As usual, the warm power washed over me like stepping into a warm waterfall. A light breeze stirred the baby hairs surrounding my face despite being indoors, and a small smile crept over my face. Stronger than LaDonna's faucet flow, this was a driving force that longed to be used. The feel of the Source surrounded me, enfolded me, filled me.

I allowed the energy to flow from my core through my limbs to my hands and fingers, and I nudged it into Hanna and Conall, willing it to fill them, rush through them, and continue pouring into the rest of the coven.

I heard Hanna's brief gasp and Conall's deep, quick laugh. I sensed their hearts opening to the love and power of the Source and bathing their souls in it. For the first time, I directed knowledge to them, understanding how to open their hearts wider to the Source and its power, and then how to push that to the person next to them.

Now it wasn't just me sharing; it was Conall and Hanna as well. As they shared the power and knowledge with those on their side, the force swelled and strengthened as it spread.

Drawing all of my focus into myself now, I felt the flow as it moved, but attuned myself to the rest of the room as well. I considered the feel of the wood below my shoes, the buzzing electricity in the bulbs around the room, the hearts pumping and brainpower zapping through coven members, my spirit and how it all connected —all of it, energy waiting to channel.

As I focused on every pair of feet on the floor touching that wood, I sent fingers of energy through my feet as well, through the planks along the floor, until we were all bound, hand to feet, in the Source. Gradually, the flow turned into a flood of love and kinship, and spirit. My entire being felt luminous, as if I could float from the floor if I only wished it enough.

A voice to my left hummed in a vibration with which they connected. Others joined, while some stayed silent with me, appreciating the flood of love and unity.

I don't know how long we stayed that way, but in time, it was time to gradually taper the power to a light flow. I didn't want to sever it, though. We were all connected now—bound in a way we'd never been before. I wanted that part to remain, for the familiarity with using the Source to go home with them.

These people had agreed to help me. The one who had always stayed on the outskirts. The one who had stayed away. They had agreed to help me, the one who had kept them at arm's length and who'd never truly thought of them as family. After twenty-six years of watching from the outside, of sitting on the outskirts staying silent when I did join them, all I had to say was that I needed help, and they decided as one to offer support.

Focusing on the cauldron, I imagined it as a vast, cooling sea, taking the heat of the Source power and cooling it, encompassing it, becoming home to it. The intensity of the energy that joined us dwindled to a light stream, and I envisioned each of us taking a portion of the power to linger in us. Separate, but strong.

We stood in the circle, joined, but now individual in our potential. No one moved. I realized I would have to be the one to break the chain, and I released Hanna and Conall's hands.

Dazed, high on Source power, the coven sluggishly let go of one another's hands. Joey was the first to speak.

"What the fuck was that?"

I laughed despite myself. "The Source."

"Yeah, but—" he stammered, motioned to where everyone was moving dreamily to the seats they'd occupied before, "I've never done anything like that before. Have you?" he turned to the rest of the coven, who were shaking their heads.

"You can now," I said.

"Not like that," Joey disagreed.

"Well… close. You have it with you now. Feel it?"

I saw heads around LaDonna's darkened living room nodding.

Joey looked at Conall and Hanna with sharp eyes that bordered on accusing. "Has she always had that power?"

Conall confirmed that, although strength of that magnitude was new, this was normal for me, and Joey sputtered at the idea that I'd stayed away from the Lughaidh coven for so long.

Conall took my hand, and I thought of how I'd shared that power our first night together. A trace of Source energy sparked through me, not unlike a second orgasm, and I trembled at the unexpected surge. Flickers of the power passed to Conall where our hands connected, and he gave me the intimate smile that made me weak.

Maybe it was time to tap into the power when we were alone together again.

Luke drew a small wooden drum from his chair and tapped it with a regular, soothing rhythm. The shift of a skirt from across the room pulled my attention to LaDonna, who, unlike the others, didn't seem drained. I asked LaDonna for some glasses for everyone, and she directed me to a sideboard where she stored some for ritual purposes. I dipped each glass into the clan cauldron, gathering a measure of water, which I delivered to each coven member to help restore their energy. The priestess joined me in dipping and providing glasses to everyone.

Over time, the coven dispersed, each with at least one jar of Source-charged water and a caution not to use it frivolously. Conall and I took our time before we left—a first for me, who in the past had always hit the door as soon as proceedings wound down. Finally, it was down to four of us—Hanna, LaDonna, Conall, and me. LaDonna's forest-green eyes took in the way Conall's hand twined with mine, my head on his shoulder, and I guessed from her motherly smile that she approved.

Chapter 18

For the next couple of days, I spent more time interacting on the group chat with the kids than I typically did so I could gauge Betony's emotional state. As I predicted, she moved on to a new significant other—an unassuming, androgynous, sweet young man named Noah—within a couple of days of Amber's breakup, but her feelings for Amber lingered. Although she flooded the chat with pictures and videos of her with Noah smiling, posing, and going to trendy places, underneath, I sensed an underlying current of heartache and rejection motivating her to advertise her happiness.

Maybe Betony's feelings had the potential to run deeper than a tablespoon.

"Hanging at Beacon's Mill!" she posted, sharing a picture of her and Noah swinging together on the oversized rope swing inside the former textile mill, now a giant arts facility. Betony loved the arts, but the big smile on her face didn't reflect in her melancholy hazel eyes the way it had been in her pictures with Amber.

Meanwhile, LaDonna spent her evenings after Witch's Brew closed helping me to understand Summates more. This turned out to be more difficult than I expected; there wasn't a lot known about them. Historically, only a handful had existed, and most written documentation about them read more like rumor or opinion.

The first night's lesson, the shop had just closed when I heard LaDonna's confident rap on the glass of the door. I greeted her and inhaled the sweet autumn air as I smiled at my high priestess, her arms laden with large, old books and her enormous cotton tote bag slung over her shoulder.

Conall strode to my side and, seeing LaDonna burdened with her massive volumes, stepped forward to relieve her. LaDonna raised her eyebrows at me and gave me a knowing look, and I, not having any way to dispute her assumption, found my cheeks coloring. Conall had come by after his day job working construction and had spent the past two evenings at my house, sticking around under the premise that he would take on the guise of Rolf, should Betony arrive. Betony never arrived, but his evenings had grown into nights spent sometimes sleeping, but often not. I should have been exhausted, but I found that channeling the Source during our lovemaking left me more charged, focused, and confident of, well, everything.

The oddest things fell into place constantly now. It was as if my intuition had grown and now bordered on faultless. Things like pricing stock had become wonderfully simple, and numbers calculated themselves in my head. My instinct was flawless when offering suggestions to people who didn't know what they were looking for—even deciding when the best time to head inside to use the restroom was intuitive. Those seem like modest instances, perhaps, but given my self-quarantined life over the years, they felt tremendous.

"Are you all right if Conall is here for our discussion?" LaDonna asked, but the question was rhetorical. She took in my nod and asked where Conall should set the books.

"Upstairs, please," I told him, "In my... room." Conall knew what I called it, but referring to my room of power as a Room of Power around LaDonna sounded juvenile. Did proper witches call the places they did their spell casting a Room of Power? I realized, to my embarrassment, that I didn't know. LaDonna's entire world was her power place; she cast wherever she went. She was a green witch who said spells by the stream when she gathered flowers. She said thanks to trees as she plucked fruit. She even thanked the animals she cooked for dinner for their sacrifice. My room of power was special to me, the one place I felt safe to be myself, to allow myself to free my ability to its fullest extent. When I was there and channeled the Source, it seemed more significant than just my room, grander than my house. It felt as if everything from the stars to specks of dust flowed through me into my spells and incantations.

LaDonna had sent me home from the coven meeting with an armload of books with the instructions to research previous stories about Summates or people who had come to be thought of as Summates by witches in history. The results had not been encouraging. I'd only found three legends of post-classical or early modern era tales of Summates and grays.

In *Early Modern History of the European Witch,* I found a tale from the 1690s of a gray born in Chalais, a small town neighboring the city of Loudon, France. The gray—a young woman named Gilet Ballouhey—came into the influence of her power as she reached adulthood. The village thrived when Gilet's role as an informal counselor to the village's problem wives abounded. Soon, however, a connection was made between the improved attitude of "hysterical females" and the misfortunes of their spouses. The Summate in this story, Marguitte

Raimbault, was known for her skills as a healer, midwife, and herbalist, and was often called on to perform handfastings and blessings on village infants. Marguitte learned about the trail of trouble linking Gilet to the village deaths and disasters and tried to confront her, but Gilet and the women she'd abetted took Marguitte's life.

The second incident took place in Turkey during the later Ottoman Empire. The details on this one were sketchy, though. The historian had gathered a tale of two powerful townsfolk—men, this time—who had opposing views on handling town crime. The reason for the lack of details was that the legend was handed down by the few townspeople who survived when the rest of the town was wiped out. I genuinely doubted the Summate caused the destruction, but neither the Summate nor the gray survived.

Not an inspiring start.

Night three of training. The shop was closed and, based on the number of books she'd brought with her tonight, it was going to be another night of reading. I tried to hide my disappointment. While understanding history was important, I failed to see how it would help me help Betony—especially if all it proved was that she'd win in the end.

After a late meal of sandwiches and chips, LaDonna and Conall headed upstairs to my room of power. I was still feeling a little disappointed by the prospect of another night of reading and allowed more space than usual between my former foster mother and me. Conall, sensing my discomfort, stayed close as LaDonna led us upstairs. Without saying a word, he took my hand and gave me a gentle smile that soothed my soul more than anything he could have said. His wide smile and his encouraging presence at my side strengthened me.

He let my hand go before we reached the top of the staircase, and I appreciated that he allowed me to stand on my own before LaDonna. Whatever was going on, I needed to draw on my strength, not his.

My footsteps lightened as I crossed the threshold to the room where I performed my spell casting. My skin tingled, and I drew in a deep breath, inhaling the mélange of fragrances of oak leaves, chrysanthemums, apples, squash, and pumpkins from my Samhain altar. In less than the time it took to complete the breath, my energy grew tenfold.

LaDonna took a place across the table from me, near one of the floor-to-elevated-ceiling bookshelves. Conall sat in a plush floral chair on the opposite side of the room, beyond my eyesight but not absent.

"Murphy, where do you keep your oils?"

I pointed to the desk and its plethora of small cubbies where I kept my oils and herbs stored in alphabetical order.

"My knee has been bothering me with all of this weather," she said. "Would you be so kind as to make me a blend?"

What weird Mr. Miyagi shit is this? I thought, but I headed to the desk, where I withdrew arnica, marshmallow root, and a few other necessary items to form a salve. I took my time blending the ingredients, breathing in the pineapple and sage smell of the arnica and the slightly vanilla marshmallow root odor. I sensed the power in each and willed the particles of them to come together in harmony, to infuse the final product with the potential to ease LaDonna's pain and relieve her inflammation.

Once done, I wiped my hands on towels I kept in a drawer nearby and poured the final product into a squat glass jar, which I presented to LaDonna. She accepted the mixture with a small smile.

"One more thing before we begin tonight," she said. She pushed one of the enormous tomes across the table at me: *The Hidden History of Magick and Alchemy.* "I need you to find the page where the story about Summates begins."

I reached across the table, but LaDonna stopped me with an outstretched palm.

"Without your hands," she finished.

Shit. I hated telekinesis. It was the weakest of my abilities—one I'd never displayed in front of anyone but Hanna, and that only alone in her bedroom after we'd had shared a stolen bottle of pinot grigio from her mother's wine rack when we were fifteen. It wasn't one I often used because it struck me as a weird combination of showy and lazy. It made little sense to draw items to oneself when a quick walk across the room took so much less mental and spiritual energy. I did use it every once in a while, to pop a door open when my hands were full, but only far enough to catch it with my foot. From there, I used physical strength.

LaDonna had not only asked me to move the pages, but she'd also asked me to detect which ones included information about Summates. She had to know how much I hated this task; I have no poker face, and besides, LaDonna was an empath. I didn't doubt the firm set of my mouth and shoulder slump resonated with her as much as the abrupt fall in my energy level. I pulled in another deep breath, this time catching a whiff of the cinnamon sticks with the other autumnal ingredients on my altar.

I am a Summate, I told myself, not yet believing it, *and this is my Room of Power.* I recalled potent spells I'd performed over the years; the tincture I'd created that eased influenza, healing a broken wrist for a hurting customer, the love spell for a couple recovering from pre-marital infidelity. I remembered how my heart soared when the ceiling seemed to melt away as I searched the heavens for signs of what was to come.

And without a word of instruction, it occurred to me: *this is easy.*

In the past few days, I had channeled the Source during multiple bouts of lovemaking and had used it to open and bond an entire coven with wisdom they had never held before.

Even if you aren't the Summate, you can do that.

A hint of a smile replaced the frown I'd tried to suppress. Would drawing on the Source be cheating? More importantly, did I care if it was? I hated how telekinesis drained me; it was a soul-exhausting effort to channel that much energy in a human body. If the power was accessible by any soul who knew how, who was I to deny myself? LaDonna had said no hands, not no Source.

Stretching my hands forward, I took in my stubby fingernails, worn down to my fingertips from years of hard work. I saw the freckles on my arms past my rolled-up flannel shirtsleeves and the Claddagh ring Conall had given me for my twenty-first birthday, the emerald heart now pointed toward my body.

I closed my eyes. If I was going to do this, I wanted it to be fast. Quick enough that LaDonna didn't have the time to tell me to handle the task without tapping into the Source. The past few days with Conall, I'd explored that power extensively. I'd enjoyed sharing that strength with him and feeling the way the power ebbed and flowed between our bodies, but also allowing my spirit to roam in the flow of it. Not to the point that I was astral projecting or lucid dreaming while tapped to the flow, but enough that the Source felt like a friend instead of an intimidating stranger. Sensing how it was part of me, but was also a part of everything.

It was part of the book in front of me.

I didn't lift the cover, never moved from the two hands extended posture I'd assumed, my eyes closed and yet seeing. If LaDonna and Conall watched without *seeing,* all they saw was that I stood there willing the book to open to the right page, hoping that I'd be able to sense the time to pause.

Instead, I was a poised lioness, ready to pounce. My spirit tiptoed around LaDonna like a thief, probing at the edges of my high priestess's knowledge in a way I'd never dared before. I learned now that I could tap more of the Source than she could, which I'd already suspected. I had more power, more strength in my spirit, more empathy, more innate ability than she'd been born with. Regardless, I respected her position as the high priestess of the clan and as my former foster mother.

Respect or not, I hated telekinesis.

LaDonna didn't detect me tiptoeing around her awareness, didn't sense me using a faint trickle of Source knowledge to finger through the book before me. I didn't see the contents of the pages so much as I experienced them, fingers of Source power touching and reading the contents with lightning speed without lifting the cover.

Summate... Summate...

There. Page forty-seven.

I released a small, single laugh through my nose. I imagined my power putting a fingernail under the page and tapped into a bit more of the ability. Effortlessly, the cover and pages flipped from right to left, and most of the pages flipped back to the right again. The book hadn't been read much, and the spine wasn't as flexible as a new volume, so the pages assumed their closed position. The cover hovered, not quite open, not quite closed.

I felt LaDonna had busted me trying to skate through a footrace. I nervously met her eyes, but instead of seeing disappointment, she waited with raised eyebrows, her expression saying, "Well?"

OK. So, she'd expected me to do it this way.

I pulled a bit more of the power into me and sent unseen fingers through the book again, found page forty-seven, and drew it open using the Source power rather than my own. I imagined a hand, fingers splayed, holding the book wide. Rather than using muscular control, the Source felt more like channeled air or an unseen push of water keeping the pages apart and the spine stretched.

Whatever. My soul wasn't tiring with the effort. That was what mattered to me.

No one spoke for a moment. The flow of the Source streamed unforced, free. Without turning, I detected Conall's attentiveness behind me, and LaDonna tapped into her Source power to better gauge the control I'd used. After giving her a moment to examine, I extended a hand to the book to keep the pages open and released my contact with the Source.

"Here," I said. "The Summate pages are here."

"They are," LaDonna agreed. "You can release the book now."

Suppressing the urge to huff in frustration the way Conall did when he was in doggy form, I dropped my hand to the side and let the pages flop back together. LaDonna used a hand to push the cover closed but said nothing. Her hand rested there a moment, fingers splayed, three fingers decorated with silver rings holding stones of opal, labradorite, and lapis lazuli. After a moment of staring at the cover of the book as if expecting it to spell out an answer, she let it go.

"Do you have a scrying mirror?" she asked.

"I-um..."

"She uses mine if she needs one," Conall's voice said from behind me. "She doesn't have her own." I nodded.

"Do you have it downstairs in your room?" LaDonna asked.

Conall said he did and unfolded his tall frame from the plush chair to retrieve it. Meanwhile, LaDonna withdrew two white taper candles and holders from her voluminous purse and a bag of rectangular wooden sticks that I recognized as palo santo from the smell. I pulled my tiny iron incense cauldron from within my desk and placed it between the candles, then moved around the room and drew the burgundy curtains closed. It wasn't necessary to block out the night, but I preferred a closed room to feel safe opening my third sight.

"What do you want me to look for?" I asked as LaDonna withdrew a lighter from a pocket hidden in the folds of her capacious skirt.

"Betony," she replied. "Look for direction regarding her and her abilities with chaos power." I received no further explanation.

Conall arrived with his scrying mirror—a plain, shiny black surface surrounded by a rectangular silver rim. Taking in the table's layout, he placed the mirror in the center of the candles, below the cauldron and nearest to me. I took a seat in front of it, across from LaDonna, and she struck the lighter and held the chunk of palo santo underneath.

"Vide, discernere, comprehende ... Vide, discernere, comprehende ..."

See, discern, understand. Over and over, she chanted the words. Conall joined her, his deep voice subdued. I let the words wash over me and fixed my gaze on the candle to the left of the mirror, allowed my stare to soften, my mind to open. LaDonna and Conall held me in their safe circle, Conall behind me, LaDonna before me. I closed my eyes, the light of the candle trapped in my mind's eye, the flame glowing and dancing.

When my psychic sight opened, I opened my eyes again and fixed my stare on the mirror. I didn't look at it so much as looking past it and allowing my meditative third eye to see into it. Shadows emerged at first, and bright spots came from the ceiling behind me, but as I unfocused my gaze, the shapes evolved, shifted, contorted.

My intellect tried to intercept the path with thoughts I'd harbored about Betony and force it into shapes I believed to be accurate, but I squelched it into silence, clearing my mind. Harboring any preconceived notions inhibited my third eye from seeing what *was*.

Betony… Betony… Betony…

I saw her in the mirror's blackness. Betony, eyebrows raised, mouth open in a startled and insulted expression. The immediate defensive wall of words flowed from her mouth. I couldn't hear them, but I didn't have to—the way she leaned forward while protecting her body with her arms crossed around her ample chest spoke enough. I saw her devolve into a black twister, shadows encompassing her as she grew. In the mirror, her physical form expanded, symbolizing the power she took to herself as she twisted and turned like a tornado, destroying anything she touched. When her face appeared in the shapes again, I expected her to appear apologetic, but instead, she owned her power, and swelled until she burst like an overfed tick. Everything below her melted like wax into misshapen puddles.

Then it was just a mirror reflecting the room and Conall behind me.

I didn't realize how shallow and slow my breath had gotten until I sucked in an enormous gulp of air and let it out gradually. Conall laid his hands on my shoulders, aware that I was out of my reverie. I took a few more breaths in silence, letting the images filter through my now fully present mind. LaDonna and Conall stood in polite silence.

"Was it successful?" LaDonna asked after a long quiet. "Did you see Betony?"

I nodded, but moved from a nod to a slow shake of my head. I raised a hand to my forehead to cradle my skull, overwhelmed. "It was Betony. LaDonna, I have no doubt she's not going to deal with it well." My stomach heaved as I recalled the effect the Betony in the mirror had on the objects below her. What did the waxy shapes represent? Her friends? Her family? The entire town of Gryphon? *Dammit, why can't these answers be more straightforward?*

"In what way?" Conall asked, crouching next to me, so he was closer to my height and looked me straighter in the face. He placed a steadying elbow on the table and another hand on the back of my chair.

"She... revels in it," I said. "She is defensive at first but then embraces it and pulls all this negative power into herself. She got so destructive." My voice dwindled off as the emotional impact of what I'd seen hit me full force: Betony swelling into a devastating power.

"Can a gray learn to control their destruction?" I asked as I jerked upright, my hand falling away from my face. "Is it possible? Controlled chaos?" Conall, trying to offer his calm, placed a palm on my jiggling knee. The warmth of his hand sank through my jeans to my leg, and I slipped back into my chair.

LaDonna leaned forward and rested her hands on the table in front of her, leaning on it heavily. She licked her lips in thought. "I imagine it's possible," she admitted.

I let out a frustrated sound. If I could have slouched further without melting off my chair, I would have.

"Y'all, I saw her growing—swelling. She was sweeping everything into herself like a tornado and wrecking everything she could. If she finds out she has chaos power, it won't go well. How are we going to stop that?"

LaDonna paused and met my gaze. "We have to make sure you're stronger."

Chapter 19

We only had three days before the Samhain gathering, and every hour of the countdown felt like a clock ticking toward doomsday. La-Donna placed the coven in charge of the party—I wasn't allowed to concern myself with any detail. Instead, my job was to tap into the Source to figure out if I had any skills I'd never discovered.

Yeah. Because *that* was easy.

When the shop had quiet moments, I worked on strengthening my telekinesis. Before all the "which witch is the gray witch?" drama started, applying the ability felt lazy. Now, it felt like a possible weapon. Lifting things with my mind was a lot like using a muscle that developed with astounding speed. The other day, I'd moved pages in a book. After that came full soda cans. Then geodes of varying sizes I had displayed on shop shelves. By the end of my first day practicing, I moved a sculpture of a dragon that I'd wager weighed twenty pounds from the floor to a top shelf and back, and I felt like Rocky with his fists raised at the top of the steps in Philadelphia.

I dove into my time in the shop during the day and craved my time with Conall at night. Every morning, he left to go to work and return to his apartment for essentials. He was at the shop each evening between five and six o'clock with his hair still wet and smelling like he'd just stepped out of the shower. He'd always had a toothbrush at my place, but it moved into my bathroom, and I liked the way his blue brush looked in the cup next to my green one. In a week's time, he'd moved from a best friend who occasionally crashed in my spare room to a lover who slept in my bedroom. I guess I didn't need as much processing as I'd thought.

On the Wednesday before the party, my jangling cell phone woke me before my alarm. Wincing, I stretched a hand to my nightstand while extending my foot towards Conall's leg. I found him and hitched an ankle around his calf just as my fingertips grasped the cell and answered it. It was LaDonna.

"Can you come over this morning?" In the background, I heard the familiar sound of a spade moving dirt. I was baffled for a moment before I realized she must be using a hands-free device. LaDonna was a bit of a Luddite, and the thought of her with a Blu-tooth attached to her ear as she gardened made me grin.

"For how long?" Conall's brown eyes flicked open, and he gave me a sleepy smile before reaching a strong arm around my waist and pulling me closer.

"A few hours, I think. Maybe the morning," LaDonna replied. What sounded like rocks hitting the metal bottom of a wheelbarrow came next.

"My shop—"

"Conall can handle it, can't he?"

He could. He'd done it in the past when I'd been sick with the flu, and Hanna had helped out so I could run errands or get haircuts. I looked at Conall's handsome face and found him looking at me with a cocked eyebrow, morning stubble making his face yet more masculine and delicious. LaDonna's voice had traveled on the quiet morning air.

"Can you?" I asked. He nodded, rolling onto his side and moving his hand on my hip, his other arm tucked under a pillow supporting his head. God, he had great arms. I used my free hand to caress his tattoo.

"How soon do you need me there?" I looked over my shoulder and eyed my clock. It was seven-thirty. The shop didn't open for another hour and a half.

"Nine o'clock? Nine-thirty?"

Half an hour to drive across town to LaDonna's house, another half an hour, maybe forty-five minutes to get ready. "Sure, I can do that."

We exchanged goodbyes, and I replaced the phone on the nightstand.

"Nine-thirty, huh?" Conall asked.

I rolled back to face him. His eyes had that look in them I knew very well.

"Yup."

He grabbed my hips and tugged me close. I wrapped my legs around him and forgot about LaDonna for the moment.

$$)O(($$

It was the first time in recent memory that I arrived at LaDonna's home without several other cars taking up most of the space in the driveway before her house which can best be described as treehouse cathedral. For coven events, I arrived late and had to park in the slot farthest from her door. Today, I slid the Corolla next to LaDonna's vintage Mercedes. I killed the engine and allowed myself a moment of silence with my eyes closed and my head resting against the seat.

I wasn't dreading the lesson, but it would be my first lesson with a head full of new ideas, most of them confusing as hell. I was a Summate, and Betony was a gray with dangerous unidentified talents.

I had to up my skills quickly and learn everything I could about my new power and Betony's to ensure mine was the stronger of the two. That her presence had weakened my wards—however unwittingly—enough to allow the gunman into my shop said volumes about her destructive potential.

The clock on my dash said nine. I pulled the keys out and exited the car, my body heavy with these problems as I walked to LaDonna's double door. Two large yellow chrysanthemums bloomed on either side in low black planters. I had to grin at the sound of her doorbell—she'd had it custom made to play a harp strumming sound.

She answered the door with a smile, a large apple green apron with a trowel and tine rake in the pockets hung over her wide slacks. She'd covered her hair with a wide-brimmed hat to keep the sun from her face. Her fingernails had half-moons of dirt under them. LaDonna avoided gloves when she gardened when she could, preferring the feel of the soil and leaves on her hands whenever prickers or thorns weren't involved.

"Good morning, Murphy!" she sang. "It's a beautiful day outside. We'll start today's lesson in the garden."

She led me past the cathedral windows to the French doors that opened to her expansive patio and backyard at the foot of a large wooded hill. She was closing her garden for the season, and a large wheelbarrow held the remains of uprooted plants and branches of perennials. The air carried a bouquet of turned earth, autumn, and fading chlorophyll. It was one of my favorite smells in the world, and it lifted the weight that held down my spirit. I recalled spending October days helping her fill her wheelbarrow, my smaller, younger hands covered protectively in rubber-palmed gloves, a pruner in one hand and a fistful of perennial branches in the other.

LaDonna saw my appreciation of the yard in my face, and her eyes sparkled. "Are you ready?"

I nodded, a smile forming on my stiff face.

She headed to the koi pond at the far end of the space, and I followed. The koi, sensing our arrival, swam to the edge and bobbed to the surface that sparkled in the morning sun, begging for food, their mouths opening and closing greedily. LaDonna gave her aquatic babies a doting smile and fetched a couple of handfuls of feed from a hidden spot under the cushion in the seat facing the pond. She nudged me with her elbow and handed me a fistful of feed to toss to the fish. I threw a few pellets in the water, and the koi gobbled up the treat in a flurry of fins and mouths and came back for more.

"Tell me about the earth and water," LaDonna said, and I smiled, recalling the lesson from my childhood.

"Earth cradles the water," I began, sprinkling the last of my pellets on the shimmering surface and rubbing my hands together to brush the crumbs into the water. "Earth cradles water, and water allows things on the earth to grow, both flora and fauna."

"Correct. And air?" She began scattering her food into the tiny pond, and the koi moved as one wiggly body in her direction.

"Air moves the water in waves and carries water from the earth's surface to the clouds, which in turn rain on the land. It blows through plants and carries their seeds and spores to grow in different places. It carries birds and insects, which spread the seeds and pollen of the earth. In the space beyond the air we breathe, the moon pulls the earthly tides."

"And at the heart of it all?"

"Is the fire of the sun. Millions of miles away, it can hurt and burn us if we are careless. We need it to grow the plants we eat and produce the oxygen in the air we breathe. The light of the sun illuminates the moon that provides light at night. The light of other stars provides nautical and astrological direction."

"What binds all of this together?"

"Spirit, what you taught me to call the Source. The energy field within everything. We are a part of it, and it is a part of us. It's in the energy we use to light candles. It's the power in the stones we use in our spells, in the water we use for ceremonial cleansing. It is the Source of all things."

She brushed the flakes of food from her hands, wiped her hands on her apron, and regarded me with a similar tender gaze as the one she'd given the koi moments ago, one of pride and love. "You remembered."

I scoffed and squatted, extending my hand toward the pond. The koi, used to human contact, tickled my fingertips looking for more food. "You drilled it into my head, LaDonna. How could I forget?"

She put a comforting hand on my shoulder and squeezed it. "Do you know what makes this lesson extra special to you?"

I thought for a moment, stood, and shrugged.

"You have a greater command of all of those elements than anyone, Murphy. You just have to believe in yourself and in your spiritual power."

"The Source."

Her dark green eyes crinkled at the corners as she smiled. "The Source."

☽○☾

LaDonna found a spare pair of gloves for me, and I squatted down near her and started trimming back the plants and clearing a portion of the garden for the season. The smell of earth and plants and crisp autumn air filled my nose and lungs and lifted my spirits. An arm's length away, LaDonna grasped branches with her bare hands, clipping and tossing the discards on top of the wheelbarrow pile. Tilting my head, I studied the experienced movement of her hands as they worked. Her actions weren't so much laboring as caressing and loving the plants.

Curious, I tugged the gloves from my hands and reached for the dried hosta stalks before me barehanded. Instead of seeing of them as dead and useless, I imagined them down to the roots and the cells and sensed the energy that had lived in them. I noticed the influence of the tired cells to discharge the strength that kept them alive, sending it to the remaining plant under the earth for it to return in spring.

I pulled, and it was like clipping the dead-end of a fingernail. The living part of the plant remained hidden under the ground.

It was then I caught LaDonna studying me nearby.

"You sense it," she observed. "The life that remains."

Stupefied by my discovery, I nodded. *So, this is what green witchery feels like.* For a moment, the urge to try and stir life back into the plant was tempting, but it went against the cycle of life. This was the dark, dying season. Maybe in the spring, I could come back and coax some extra life into them.

"It's all part of the balance," she said, as if she'd sensed my thoughts. "The death of the flowers is part of the life cycle of the hosta, like the falling tree leaves. Nature has her way during the long, dark nights of the year just as she does the long days of summer."

I remembered how only a few days ago, I thought I was chaos personified. Now, I had the power of earth, air, fire, water, and spirit to wield. The knowledge was heady.

"Do you think... When you and Hanna and Conall came to my house that night, you said chaos has a purpose. The Universe brings a gray into a place for a reason."

"Yes, I believe so."

"What could the reason be? I've been living for years like a hermit, when I could have been helping Betony. What purpose does that serve?"

She shook her head and put her tools down, sitting cross-legged on the earth to face me. "I don't know, Murphy. Betony arriving in Gryphon set your powers on an unexpected trip of reflecting her gray powers instead of coming into your own. Perhaps you had to learn how to restrain the power of the gray."

"I never learned how to do anything with that power, though. I don't know how to live anything other than self-defense and isolation. And now that I know I'm the Summate, everything's going to be peachy-keen?"

"I never said that things would be peachy," she said disapprovingly. "However, I do think that perhaps there's a reason the Universe needed you to close off for a time."

I scoffed as a tense smile crossed my face. To my surprise, my vision blurred as my eyes grew hot with tears. "Like what? The Universe didn't want me to have a social life? To go to public high school? To get laid?"

LaDonna's reproving expression, one hand cocked on her hip, was scolding enough. "Perhaps the world wasn't ready to have an emotional teenager with boundless elemental power in the same town as a new baby with a different ability she couldn't possibly know about, much less control."

My downcast eyes found the pulled hosta stalks, and heavy tears landed on the withered leaves. I tossed them on top of the garden rubbish. My cheeks were burning, and it wasn't from the blustery autumn wind.

"I was pretty emotional, wasn't I?" I admitted with a dry chuckle.

LaDonna's throaty laugh made me a little less ashamed of my outburst. "You were pretty bad, but I've seen worse."

Flopping down on my bottom, I turned to face my foster mother, assuming a cross-legged seat as well.

"What do I do, LaDonna?" I asked plaintively.

She gave me a meager smile. "Without a little chaos, the universe would die of entropy. You can balance her if she lets you. Your power is greater."

"Yeah, but *how?*"

She took my hand in hers. Hers were weathered and calloused but also solid and reassuring. "Practice in the little things, and grow into the big ones. Let the Universe guide you, Murphy. It will always tell you the right thing to do."

Chapter 20

My confidence bolstered after my visit with LaDonna, I headed back to the house and shop, looking forward to telling Hanna and Conall about my productive morning. As I maneuvered the Toyota down the woodsy winding roads leading from LaDonna's house, my phone pinged, alerting me to a group message. I caught Betony's name from the screen before the message disappeared from view. For once, it didn't have a photo, video, or a GIF in it.

Whatever it is must be pretty serious.

I waited until I reached a stoplight before checking my phone. The message was a short one.

Bet: *Mama Murph, can you teach me how to make a sour jar?*

I frowned and tossed the phone back into the cupholder. Betony wanted to hex someone, and I was willing to wager dollars to donuts that it was Amber.

The light turned green, and I cussed myself for looking at the message before I had time to respond. Now my chat head had moved down, so Betony knew I had read her question but wasn't answering. She probably guessed I was avoiding giving her an answer. Which, to be fair, I would have even if I wasn't driving.

I didn't like that Betony had decided to take it upon herself to sour someone's life. Hexes and curses should never be taken lightly. I don't believe in the Rule of Three the way Wiccans do, but I trust the energy that one puts into the universe will influence the returned energy. As far as I knew, the only crime Amber had committed was breaking up with Betony—nothing worthy of a sour jar.

You can't be sure it's Amber that Betony wants to sour. Wait until you have all the facts before jumping to conclusions.

I waited until I hit another light before snagging my phone and hitting voice text. "Who do you want to sour? That's not something to take lightly, you know." I hit send and slammed the phone back into the cupholder. It pinged almost immediately.

Bet: *I'm not planning to sour anyone. I just want to learn how that's all. A friend at school was asking if I knew how, and I thought I should.*

The light turned green, and I brought my hands back to the wheel to consider my response. *Asking for a friend.* I scoffed. How stupid did she think I was? I flashed back to the seven of swords card from the tarot reading I had done the day my shop was almost robbed, when the universe had warned me about a deceptive person coming into my life.

I had one more traffic light before I hit the main thoroughfare, and it was a long one. I sighed, picked up my phone, and hit voice text again. "I'm not sure you're ready for sour jars yet, Bet." I thumbed the *send* button and turned my attention to the traffic. Again, I received an almost immediate ping.

Frowning, I lifted my phone. Two large, teary-eyed emojis looked back at me. I rolled my eyes and put the phone back. Cadence and Jake had warned me this might happen. Too bad I hadn't prepared a response in advance.

If she assumes I'm going to teach her how to ruin someone's life over a break-up grudge, she's got another think coming. I followed a Tundra through the green light and forced my jaw to relax. There were probably fewer more dangerous in the world than a gray Scorpio witch with a break-up grudge. No. Freaking. Way.

Then again, wasn't it my responsibility as both her teacher and the Summate to make sure she didn't use her power irresponsibly? If I didn't guide her, I left her open to trying any careless spell and hex she found on the internet or heard secondhand from some rebellious goth at school who considered themselves a witch because they wore eyeliner and refused to attend church.

Sour jar spells were easy to find—any internet search would tell her how to put one together. What they might not explain, though, was the ramifications of making one. The spiritual consequences and the impact on one's conscience left one open for one hell of a karmic rebound. As her informal instructor, the Summate, and, dare I say it, her friend, it was my job to ensure her safety. God help Amber if she succeeded.

Amber? Try the whole town! An angry, untrained gray assembling a sour jar can create the spell equivalent of an undirected bomb. Shit on a shingle. What do I do now?

)O(

Middays on Wednesdays were never a busy time for Witch's Brew, and even though the sky was cloudless and the weather a few degrees warmer than it had been, today was no exception. After the handful of lunchtime visitors had taken their leave, Conall and I put together our favorite brews and steered ourselves to seats between the register and the front of the shop, where we could keep an eye on the door.

"You said it went well at LaDonna's," he began, as he took a seat across from me at one of the smaller circular tables. "But something's been bugging you since you got back—you haven't been able to sit still. What is it?"

I studied the layer of mocha foam on the top of my thick porcelain mug. "It's Betony. She asked me how to make a sour jar."

He grimaced, and I found his wrinkled nose adorable. "What'd you tell her?"

I shrugged. "I told her the truth. That she's not ready for sour jars yet."

"She's not," he agreed. He took a sip from his favorite mug, one with a rainbow parade of Grateful Dead bears dancing on its side. "How'd she take it?"

"She lied. At least, I think she did. Said she wanted to learn because someone at school asked her about it, and she felt like she should know how they're done."

He snorted mid-sip and about sprayed me with coffee. After collecting himself, he replied, "Yeah," drawing the word out skeptically as he sat back and slung an elbow over the back of his chair. "I'm not buying that, either."

"I need to give her enough to keep her satisfied, though," I said. "If I don't, and she's hell-bent on learning, there's no telling what sketchy shit she'll find on the internet or whatever. And if she's hurt and plans on directing her focus on a sour jar spell, Goddess knows the chaos she could release, and neither does she. She doesn't know she's the gray yet!"

We sat in silence, mulling over the problem as we sipped our coffees and watched the door.

"How bad do you think it could get?" he asked.

I frowned. "You know all that crazy shit that happened whenever I leave here? The car problems? Jacked up GPS directions? Broken bones? Messed up food orders? Horrible, inexplicable weather?"

"Yeah?"

"That was just me reflecting the impact of her unfocused energy. Imagine if that power came straight from its home, and she focused it."

"Has she done any other spells that you know of?"

"Nothing major," I admitted. "But she did say she thinks she's the reason her bus runs late on mornings when she oversleeps a bit."

"That's not much."

"No, but it's what she's admitted to me," I took a sip of coffee. "I suspect the reason she's intrigued with the craft is because she senses something different about herself. I guess I should be glad she's asking me for guidance instead of just trusting the crap she finds on the net. What scares me is that it also means she doesn't want to fuck up the sour jar. She knows it's serious, and she has a definite intent."

Conall ticked with his tongue and contemplated. His eyes danced around the room as he thought, trying to come up with a way to keep her destruction at bay.

"Conall, it could affect more than just Amber," I said. "I'd wager she has the strength in her to put the entire town of Gryphon in danger. Like I said, if her reflections were disastrous..."

Conall leaned forward once more. "Tell you what. Why don't you astral project to her? See what she's up to? It might give you a sense of where her head is."

I shook my head, my eyes wide as tension crept into my shoulders. "You know I don't do that. I've never been able to properly."

He took my hand. "I know the idea scares you, but you always assumed you were the gray before."

I let out a dry, choked laugh. "Scares me. That's one way of putting it. Terrifies me is another."

"If you're going to help Betony, you have to be able to keep an eye on her when she starts acting shady. I could do it, but you know her better than I do. And as a Summate, it's a skill that'd be a useful one for you to master."

My mouth flattened. I saw his logic, but I still hated it. Part of it was that I hated the idea of spying on someone, but mostly I hated the idea of astral travel. Having my spirit travel outside of my body far enough to peek in on Betony on one of my first tries seemed incredibly chancy. I pulled my hand away from his and slumped heavily against the back of my seat.

"I can help you. I'll talk you through it, and I'll stay by your side the whole time so I can call you back if I need to."

Easy for him to say. To Conall, astral projection came as easily as dreaming. It tied into his prophecy gift, which allowed him to see into others' lives.

"Do you want me to travel with you?" he offered, and I balked, my hands waving in front of me.

"No. No way. I need to have you here. As an anchor."

Nodding, he took another swallow of coffee before heading around the counter to the folder of pages where I kept random receipts, catalogs, and purchase orders. He withdrew a plastic clock with poseable arrows that said "WILL RETURN AT" in bold letters at the top and strode to the front door, positioning the clock's arms as he walked.

"What—now?" I asked, startled.

"Yes," he replied. "If Betony is going to look into how to make a jar, she'll do it today, don't you think? And soon, if she hasn't started already."

He was right. If she was curious, she'd been researching on her phone whenever her classes allowed and planned to create one as soon as she got home. Sour jars didn't need complicated ingredients—most folks had the equipment at home.

He found the suction cup hanger from its hiding place on a shelf near the door and stuck the clock in place. He withdrew his keys from the front pocket of his jeans and locked the entrance to the shop. Heading back purposefully, he extended a hand in my direction.

"Come on," he insisted. "Let's do this."

I swallowed hard, took one last sip of coffee, and accepted his hand. Together, we headed through the double doors into my home.

We reached the kitchen, and Conall hesitated. "Do you want to take a moment and try to relax? Have some tea? We shouldn't wait too long, school will be out soon, but if that would help—"

"Hell no," I said. "The longer we put this off, the more time I'll have to work myself into a tizzy. Let's go ahead and fucking do it."

He nodded and, still holding my hand, led me upstairs to my bedroom. This time felt so different from all the other times he had accompanied me there. The butterflies in my stomach weren't from excitement, and this time I was loath to enter the bed. He told me to lie down, and as I did, reluctantly, he pulled one of the wingback chairs away from the bay window and up to my bedside. Sitting as close as possible without physically touching me, he stared down into my face, which I had no doubt reflected every last fragment of my fear. I fixed my attention on his large brown eyes and found the tension easing out of me.

"Perfect," he said, sensing my change in attitude. "Breathe for a minute. Think relaxing thoughts."

I thought of how many times he and I had spent the night tangled up in the sheets under me. Of waking up with him spooning my back. Before I knew it, a hint of a smile played at the corners of my mouth. Conall's eyes traveled to my lips, but he stayed inches away.

"Relax your body," he whispered, his breath smelling not unpleasantly of coffee. I did, willing the tension in my muscles to ease. "Can you close your eyes?" he asked. I did that as well, concentrating on my inhales and exhales. "I'm right here, baby."

He'd never called me that before, and it made my grin grow. Determined not to mess this up, I erased it from my face and pulled in a deep lungful of air, releasing it in a sigh as I willed the tightness from my body.

Slowly, and with a smooth, deliberate cadence, he spoke. Conall's voice always made me content and relaxed, anyway. Today, I allowed his melodious voice to fall over me like silk, caressing my mind and soothing my fears. The entire world became my awareness of Conall's low, flowing voice. I had a couple of odd twitches as the nerves in my body eased, but soon my breathing became deeper, my body relaxed. The blackness behind my eyelids covered me, complete and comfortable. The rhythm of my breath, my heartbeat, eased and relaxed, and then I was aloft.

One second, I was lying on the bed; the next, I was inches above it in the same position.

Conall sensed the moment I separated. Although my eyes were closed, I saw his focus twitch in my direction. Bless him, his voice changed not one iota. Calm as sunflower turning to the sun, he continued his assuring vocal patter as my spirit lifted higher and pivoted, so he stayed in view. I reached the ceiling and saw myself on the bed, my hair almost the color of dark copper spread across the pillow. I looked so relaxed.

"I got you," Conall said. "I'm right here."

I suppose it wouldn't be technically correct to say I looked, but whatever part of my spirit held the focus of my attention turned toward the window. I considered the distance from here to the high school, where Betony was—close enough that I heard the football games when the weather was right—and it felt worlds away. I imagined how pleasant it would be to fly over the village in the autumn air, looking at the brightly colored leaves. All I had to do was float toward the window and—

No!

The terror that I had suppressed crashed down over me in an enormous wave.

Go past the window? Leave your room and fly away from your body like a ghost? What am I, crazy? What if I can't come back? What if—?

"Murphy? Honey, listen to me. You're OK."

My floating persona disagreed. In a fleeting moment of panic, my spirit bolted towards my body. In that same split second of terror, it found itself drawn to the mellow sound of love and comfort and peace, longed to embrace the soul I'd known as safety and companionship from my youth. In my zeal for security, my spirit dove past the body lying on the bed and leaped into the vessel it craved.

Eyes that were not mine blinked and saw my body reclined on the bed. A heart that wasn't mine jumped in confusion, and when I willed myself to speak, it was Conall's voice that said, "Holy shit."

My heart stopped. Or maybe it was his. What had I done? I swallowed and became weirdly aware of an Adam's apple.

Oh, crap. I missed.

It's OK, Murph. We got this.

I gasped, but it was Conall who took the breath. Twin trains of thought in one mind.

This is fucking crazy, even for me.

Yes, it is. Hold on.

Even in a moment of such a novel experience, he remained placid, unflappable, and I loved him even more for it. I felt his mind willing his arm to raise and grasp my hand. As he saw my blank expression and deathly still body, a wave of his love and concern for me enveloped both of us. My... well, his... vision blurred with tears brought on by my spirit's awareness of the depth of his love for me.

Holy shit.

He chuckled, and I noticed the voice resound in my chest the way I never did with my own.

Told you, he said and took my hand. Our auras mingled, covering his body in a cornflower blue haze. Conall tapped into a trickle of the Source and directed my spirit's flow, so that my indigo energy traveled through his body and focused on his physical center. From there, my spirit, drawn by the connection to its home, flowed from his body to mine like water flowing from one glass into another. Once filled, I jerked upright with a gasp, and my eyes shot open. The room seemed darker, somehow.

Flopping back onto my mattress, I covered my eyes with my forearm. "Well, I really fucked that up."

Conall rose from the chair and kicked off his shoes to lie on the mattress next to me. "'S'allright," he said, wrapping me in his arms. "It was worth a try."

"Maybe if I pull on Source power—"

He kissed my neck, and it tickled. "Not right now. I don't want to exhaust you."

"Speaking of Source, when did you learn that little trick? I've never seen you wield the power before."

"I've never done it before."

I fought with conflicting emotions of pride in Conall for tapping into the Source and the urge to continue scolding myself for my inability to get over the fear of leaving my body. I was the Summate. What in the hell was wrong with me? If astral projecting was beyond my talents, did I stand a chance at mastering any other Summate skills? What if the talent I'd displayed inside Witch's Brew was the most I mastered my whole life?

"What do I do, Conall?"

He let out a quick laugh and kissed my hand, held tightly in his. "Call her?"

I laughed despite my tension and self-doubt. "To hell with it. I'll call her. Maybe I can talk her down off the sour jar ledge."

Conall pulled me in for a tight embrace. "You can do it."

I hope so. If not, Goddess, help the soul she wants to hurt.

Chapter 21

The bright yellow-orange high school buses driving down Oberon Street told me the high school had released for the day. I fought the urge to dial her the minute the first one passed the shop. It'd take a while for Betony to get to her house and gather the ingredients for the spell. I'd had to take her home more than once when a ride she'd counted on had fallen through and knew she lived way out in what she fondly referred to as "Yee-hawville."

After enough time had passed, I called Betony from the shop. The line rang a few times, and then a familiar, smiling face filled the screen and blocked the view of most of the room behind her. She'd dyed her hair raspberry pink since I'd seen her last, and she seemed happy to see me.

"Betony, are you busy right now?"

"Um… no," she said, the trepidation in her voice coming through the phone lines. Her eyes panned something near her feet, and I knew it could be anything from her dog to spell ingredients. "Why?"

I need to distract you, so you don't make a sour jar before you understand the importance of your actions.

"Well, I want the shop to look especially festive for this Saturday for the Samhain party. I was hoping you could put some of your artistic skills and your knowledge of the store, my products, and the craft into making it look more pretty than ever? I really want to go all out this year and maybe draw some new people in."

"Sure!" she crowed. "Will I get paid?"

I laughed genuinely; the stress of worry lifted for now at the heartened sound in her voice. "Of course. Can you come over this afternoon? And Friday, too?"

She agreed, and we said our goodbyes. If she'd planned on doing anything untoward, apparently it wasn't anything that couldn't wait until Samhain.

I sank into the bar-height chair I kept near the register, glad for once that today was a slow one. The days before Halloween were typically some of our busiest. Perhaps the Universe was looking out for me.

"Need me to go get her?" Conall offered.

"That'd be great," I agreed. "While you're gone, I'll strengthen my wards."

☽◯☾

As soon as Betony strode through the door, it was clear she was in an excellent mood. She positively radiated. Her smile was wide, her stride confident. At some point in the day, she'd made spiderwebs at the edges of her eyes with eyeliner. Her shirt showed a cycle of the moon, and below it were the words, "Not A Phase." Her boots were more youthful and high-heeled than mine and looked much more uncomfortable, but hey—with age comes experience. In my experience, Converse and Doc Martens were way more comfortable. By the time I was La-Donna's age, I'd probably be wearing moccasins like she does.

"Mama Murph!" she chirped, coming around the counter to envelop me in an enormous hug—very atypical of Betony, who normally shied away from physical affection. Behind her, Conall gave me an impressed smile. "What do you need help with?"

"Everything," I joked. "The shop is decked out for Samhain, but I'd like some more of my seasonal décor put out on the porch to draw trick-or-treaters. Nothing that might blow away or that costs too much, in case of thieves. I can restock displays inside and make sure everything is full."

We went back and forth on the details for a few minutes, settled on her fee, and she set to work with an air of confidence and genuine happiness. Conall winked at me and disappeared behind the double doors, reappearing moments later as Rolf. I bent down and scratched him behind his ears and told him to behave with a pat to his head. He gave me a wolfish smile and winked again before trotting over to follow Betony as she labored with my display of t-shirts and bohemian skirts. Betony couldn't be happier about her furry new friend trailing after her, and she paused often to scratch him on his head and chin.

Customers trickled in as workdays ended. This time of year, I was always sure to stock up on wands and capes and pointed black hats for folks who wanted to use them as props for costumes. Did I feel it was a bit like cultural appropriation of witchy culture? A little. But I would rather have folks seeing us as fun and whimsical than as evil. And the extra money didn't hurt.

Betony loved playing the part of a shop employee, guiding querying customers to displays of herbs, cauldrons, incense, and candles with a genuine smile and a "Glad I could help." Interruptions of her display work didn't put her out in the slightest, and "Rolf's" short, wolfy legs trotted alongside her with every step.

I was thankful I'd asked her to help out tonight—the store was far busier than I expected. While I was grateful for the sales, the crowd made it difficult to keep an eye on Betony. For an hour, I switched back and forth between ringing in customers and helping Betony show customers where to find the items they wanted. Invariably, there was a myriad of customer questions. Can I eat this? Is this safe to use around pets? How strongly does this candle smell when it's burning? What are the differences in quartz colors?

As I rang in one of my favorite customers—a sweet woman in her thirties named Rita who had rainbow-colored hair and multicolored tattoos—a paw pressed on my calf. Looking down, I saw "Rolf" peering at me keenly.

"What's the matter, um, boy?" I asked. Calling the dog my boyfriend's name would be a super embarrassing slip-up. *Holy cow, I have a boyfriend. How weird is that?*

"New dog?" Rita asked happily, bending down to say hello. "Rolf" allowed a dutiful greeting from the fawning human and stood for scratches for only a second before coming back and pawing my leg again.

"I'm dog-sitting," I explained.

"He must need to go out," Rita said with a smile.

"That must be it," I agreed, lifting her bags across the counter for her. "Thanks for coming in. Could you excuse me?"

I followed my furry boyfriend through the doors into my kitchen, where he trotted directly to the staircase and whined.

"Upstairs?" I asked. He nodded. If you don't think it's weird to see a dog nod and look at you with complete comprehension, let me tell you— it is.

I ascended the staircase, noticing as I did the little furball heading to a pile of disheveled clothes in the corner of my kitchen. Conall was changing back to himself, which made me a little wary of what I might find at the top.

Taking the stairs far quieter than I normally would have, I reached the topmost tread with my head swiveling like a high-speed oscillating fan. A rustling sound drew my eye to my Room of Power. Betony emerged with her backpack slung over one shoulder, a tiny stuffie from one of the more recent anime films dangling from the zipper. She was looking around about knee height, most likely looking for the dog who had gone downstairs to alert me to her mischief, so my presence didn't register immediately. Once it did, she jumped back with a startled, "Oh!"

"What are you doing?" I tried to keep the accusatory tone from my voice.

"I had to use the bathroom, and I—"

"Why didn't you go downstairs?"

"There was a customer there. So, I came up here, and I just had to look before I headed down. Your room is so pretty. That stained glass is amazing. Rolf and I were just vibing."

I eyed her and her backpack skeptically. She caught my doubtful scrutiny of her bag, and she had an explanation for that, too.

"I needed a tampon." From the moment I'd caught her upstairs, her words had an odd combination of truth and lie in them, and I struggled to tell which was which.

I hesitated a moment to collect my anger before I spoke. "Don't go in there without me again. Do you understand?"

"Yes. I do. I'm sorry."

You should be. And I don't buy for a second that you were in there just to look.

When we reached downstairs, Betony tucked her backpack into my tiny storage room and scampered dutifully back to the shop. I paused to talk to Conall, who was sitting at the kitchen island with a steaming glass of tea as if he'd been there the whole time.

"What was she doing?" I asked softly, my eyes on Betony's back as I leaned on the counter near him.

"I wish I knew. I ran down to come get you as soon as she headed to your room. The only intel I can give you is that she got a text from Amber when she was outside. After that, she headed straight upstairs like she had a goal in mind."

"My room."

He nodded.

I shook my head. "I'm going to ask her to show me what's in her bag."

He put a hand on my arm. "I've been tossing that around since you mentioned she was asking about making a sour jar. Maybe you should wait."

"Wait!" I exclaimed, "Why on earth would I wait?"

"Samhain's only a couple of days away. We should see what happens."

My stomach clenched at the image of Betony wandering around with something she had taken from my Room of Power.

"Think about it, Murphy," he said. "You've always charged the things in that room with positive power. The odds of her being able to undo that—"

"She's a *gray witch*." My hand pressed my face, pushed my eyebrows back, covered my mouth. "Just her *existing* in the town of Gryphon has had me believing that *I* was the gray for years."

He took the hand on my arm and used it to turn me in to face him. "That was before you learned you were the Summate. You're stronger, and now, you can overcome the chaos."

I considered the handful of stories LaDonna had had me read, stories about Summates throughout history and the power they wielded. I recalled the night at LaDonna's with the coven and how I'd channeled enough Source power for everyone connected to experience it. I was the Summate, but was it enough?

"You're doubting yourself," he said softly, his brown eyes finding mine.

"How could I not?"

He tried pulling me in for a hug, but I resisted. Worry lines formed between his brows. "Murphy, remember that this time you're not alone. You've always had Hanna and me and LaDonna, but you've got the whole coven, too."

The whole coven. Right.

"We're right behind you. We always have been."

I allowed myself to be embraced, but it didn't take away my concern. Betony had at the very least done some research in my spellbooks. At the worst, she'd stolen some of my equipment. I felt as if I'd opened the door to Betony's cell and had handed her a gun.

Chapter 22

Thursday and Friday passed, and other than a slightly more active chat room among the teens looking forward to Halloween, not much changed. I got to see the costumes everyone planned to wear to the party as they all exchanged pics. Jake was going to dress as a popular dark superhero who had risen from the dead, and he had surprisingly said he'd allow Cadence to dye his hair black for the day. I'm not sure who Lorina's character was supposed to be, if any. Her costume looked like a cross between a harlequin doll and a dominatrix. Cadence had assembled a stunning anime costume from articles she'd found around her house put together with others she had made or borrowed from friends at school. Betony had opted for a creepy clown that she said she'd modeled after the fans of a band she liked, and she had braided her long, pink hair into adorable braided pigtails. I learned that Noah, Betony's current fling, wouldn't be able to make it to the party, because he had to take his little siblings trick-or-treating. It looked like our hope for triggering trigger a chaos response from Betony hung entirely on Amber, and on Betony still harboring a grudge for being dumped.

Cadence and Jake had agreed to help me get Amber there, clandestinely inviting her to the party following the evening open house at the shop. We all held our collective breath to see if Amber reached out to Betony regarding the party. Either she didn't, or Betony wasn't saying. When the shop opened on Samhain morning, I had no idea if Betony suspected what we had planned for her that day.

For my costume this year, I decided to try a new outfit. Most years, I opted for the stereotypical green skin and pointy hat. This Saturday morning, I asked Conall to run the shop while Hanna and I headed for my upstairs bathroom. After slipping into her Queen of Hearts costume (fitting for a red witch, I thought), Hanna struggled with curling my hair into Glinda-like spirals while I powdered my face alabaster white to hide my freckles and slight summer tan. After she finished, I slipped on a frilly pink gown with a wide hooped bottom and topped it all off with a silvery crown to complete the illusion. The costume had come with a toy wand, but since I was running a shop and hosting a party, I would leave that upstairs with the package the gown had come in.

"Stop… fussing!" Hanna barked, pinning the crown to my head with bobby pins as I scratched at the tulle under my dress.

"It itches!"

"Don't let it! Remember what LaDonna told you. Practice in the little things—"

"And grow into the big ones. I know. I've heard it a million times." I closed my eyes and turned my attention from Hanna poking my head with the pins to the irritated skin frustrating me. I imagined it as calm, no burning, no itching. Within seconds, the urge to scratch my skin vanished. I opened my eyes, knowing the frazzled look behind them had vanished, too.

"See?" Hanna took my hand—the one that moments ago had been clawing under my dress—and squeezed it.

"I always knew you were special," she said tenderly. "You being the Summate just shows the rest of the world what I already knew—you're the best."A weak smile came over me quickly, combined with eyes ready to overflow with sentimental tears. I sucked in a deep breath and fought the urge to sob.

"Don't you dare," she warned with a pointed finger extended at my face. "I spent too much time making your eyeliner the perfect blend of smoky and subtle."

I choked out a laugh and rolled my eyes at the chandelier, wishing the tears back into my skull.

"What would I do without you?" I asked, my heart wrenched at the notion.

"Well, for one, curls in the back of your hair wouldn't look nearly so uniform."

☽○☾

Downstairs, the portion of the party taking place inside Witch's Brew had taken off with gusto. Two human-height posable plastic skeletons held a cooler of drinks for the parents, and inside I had a cauldron of mulled cider on "smoking" dry ice inside near the register. Betony and Lorina stood at the door with enormous metal buckets of candy, both fascinating and terrifying the children who'd come by trick-or-treating. "Rolf" charmed everyone, parents and kids alike, in his hellhound devil costume wings and bright red horns that LaDonna had made for him. The purple and orange lights strewn around the columns and balusters of my wide porch only succeeded in making their already creepy costumes even creepier, and the ghost "flying" from the fan looked adorably spooky.

This year's decorations included some fun new ones, including a

Ouija board that had a self-moving planchette that Conall had converted from an old skating-rink toy he'd found at someone's garage sale.

The open house included plenty of spooky goodies, including licorice string spiders, apples with fluffy caramel dip, chocolate cookies with mummy wrap icing, and a few other treats. Hanna had taken care of the cookies, and, like most of her baked goods, they were disappearing rapidly.

I grabbed a small plateful of mummy cookies and a couple of mugs of warm mulled cider and carefully headed out to the curb. I nodded to Cadence, Lorina, and Betony as I passed them. Watching my step, so I didn't tread on my skirts or splash my costume with cider on my way down the porch steps, I carried the snack past the tall hedges at the edge of my property to the squad car hidden behind them.

I knocked on the window with my elbow, and Kenny Hendricks rolled it down, his smile bright in the dark interior of the car. I passed him the mugs of cider and the plate of cookies.

"I guessed that you gentlemen might need a snack," I offered.

"Why, thank you," he replied. "You didn't have to do that."

"Sure I did. Y'all are doing me a huge favor keeping an eye on the place tonight."

Officer Stout took a bite and made an appreciative sound. "When you say there might be a problem, we're going to take that seriously, Murphy," he said around a mouthful of cookie.

"I wish I could tell you more. Honestly, at this point, it looks like my intuition might have been a bust."

Hendricks nodded understandingly, and I was grateful that he didn't seem in the least bit perturbed that his mini stake-out might have been for nothing. I supposed chilling in a cruiser downing cider and cookies beat chasing down kids TP-ing one another's houses.

"I'd better head back inside," I said. "The shop closes at eight tonight, and I don't suspect anything will happen after that."

"You sure?" Hendricks asked. "Better safe than sorry."

"Nah," I said, touched that he cared. "Don't feel like you gotta stick around after that. And thanks again."

I started to walk off when I heard Hendrick's voice call my name. I turned to catch a broad smile across his handsome face.

"You make a good Glinda," he said, and the way he stressed the words, I sensed that he *knew*. Witch's Brew wasn't a novelty shop, it was my life, and he believed that I was a good witch. I thought of the numerous times he'd had to save me from the messes I'd made, and gratitude for him understanding that it wasn't intentional swept over me.

Barely able to speak around the lump in my throat, I croaked. "Thanks, Kenny."

I headed back inside the shop, still bustling with business. Busy Halloweens are a perk of being a shop known for its offbeat and eerie vibe. Most folks bought what they viewed as innocuous items when viewed from outside the store walls, but a handful bought things I had no doubt would be used in their own Samhain celebration later that night.

"Rolf" followed Betony everywhere, his claws clicking on the hardwood store floors, and Betony doted on him almost endlessly. She hardly stopped fussing over him to pass out candy. The handful of times I managed to catch his eye, my furry man gave me the slightest headshake to signal that he hadn't sensed anything foreboding arriving soon. I wondered if being a dog hindered his gift.

Dogs have exceptional sensitivities of their own, though, and they predict earthquakes. Maybe being a dog heightens his gift.

The young trick-or-treaters started tapering off about the time the coven members began arriving, and I needed to close the store. Lorina washed off her makeup and changed from her sexy costume into a pair of black jeans and a Nirvana t-shirt, grousing the whole time about her overly strict parents before heading home for her early curfew. As Hanna and I pulled the sodas and ice out of the skeleton basin and added candy in its place for any late trick-or-treaters, I noticed the squad car pulling off. I gave the guys a wave and a salute, which they returned from their rolled-down windows.

There was still no sign of Amber, and the kids had been so busy with the party the chat had been quiet all night. If they'd gotten word from Amber about whether she was coming or not, they hadn't said. I had impressed on them the importance of keeping tabs on both Betony and Amber, and I hated to think they'd let me down.

I locked the doors, and the party moved to my kitchen and the two rear rooms of Witch's Brew—what would have been the parlor and sitting rooms had I lived in an average house. Instead, it made a friendly place for everyone to congregate and sit in the tables and chairs already in place. Adult drinks joined the sodas, and spiced rum poured into the mulled cider. Betony and the kids joined us for the after-party, but the chatter on the group text said they were planning to go to another party after they had a chance to say hello to the coven and grab some munchies.

LaDonna held court without even trying, as usual, but her eyes caught mine often, reading in my frustrated expression and tense body that I wasn't optimistic the night would go as planned now that the shop doors were closed. The window for triggering Betony's chaos energy was closing, and Amber had not shown up. After making the rounds and greeting the coven members I hadn't said hello to yet, I took a mug of mulled cider to the window and stared past my front porch and the Halloween lights to Oberon Street. A handful of children, high on sugar and night energy, danced by with an exhausted-looking parent, their voices raised and their smiles wide as they swung their bags of sugary treasures.

If it doesn't happen tonight, it's not meant to. The Universe makes everything happen when the time is right. That way, everything stays in balance—even chaos.

Perhaps Halloween was too risky a night to trigger her, with the veil between the living and dead so thin. I couldn't figure how that would matter, but I was one tiny human in a grand cosmos, and I trusted the universe to know best.

Hanna glided up to me and gave me a meek but friendly smile. She too had a mug of cider, and we toasted one another silently, eyes connected, before taking a sip.

I jumped at the sensation of fur against my leg.

"Rex!" I scolded, handing Hanna my mug before reaching under my petticoats to extract my cranky familiar. He fussed for about two seconds before submitting himself to be held and shedding black hair all over my pink gown.

"How did you figure out that Rex was your familiar?" I heard a friendly voice ask.

Betony.

Sure enough, the goth clown teen queen was striding in our direction with Rolf at her heels. She'd let down her pigtails, and her hair tumbled in raspberry waves down her back. I smiled.

Trust me, Bet; that one ain't yours.

I shrugged and set Rex down carefully. He disappeared under my petticoats again, and I shook my head.

"It wasn't as if I had a lightning strike or anything," I replied. "He just… we just bonded over time. He went from being an independent little cranky stinker to being there for me when I needed him. He cared for me when I was sad or sick. He sleeps with me. When I did my spells or wrote in my grimoire, he was there at my side. One day, I realized that I felt stronger when he was there. It was like he lent me some of his aura, his power, in whatever I did."

"And then there's the fact that he hates everyone but you," Hanna teased.

I scoffed. "Not *everyone.*"

"He's a grumpy old man," she said with a laugh. Rex poked his head out and deigned to allow Hanna to scratch his little black furry head.

"See, not *everyone.*"

Betony squatted down and extended her hand near Hanna's, but Rex wasn't having it. He hissed and jetted to the other side of the room, choosing to give his affection to LaDonna instead. He wove through her legs until she stopped her conversation to bend down and stroke from head to tail.

"He's *looking* at me," Betony pouted. She turned to Rolf, who was standing between her and me. "*You* wouldn't do that, would you?" she asked. Rolf did that adorable dog head tilt that looked so natural on him that I wondered how he did it.

"Maybe Rolf could be my familiar," Betony suggested. "He really likes me."

I smiled at her with the most paternal expression I could muster. "When you find your familiar, you'll know."

Betony's unconvinced expression left me a little uneasy.

Maybe it's time to try to talk to Betony about what type of witch she is. The coven could help me explain.

"Betony, have you met the coven?" I asked. She shook her head before dropping her chin as her arms crossed around her chest.

"Come on," I said. "You've already met a few of us—me, Hanna, Conall. You've met LaDonna." I put an arm near her back to guide her but didn't touch her, knowing how sensitive she was about human contact.

She allowed me to corral her and make introductions, her smile as disarming as ever as I introduced her around. I saw through her discomfort—the slight rounding of her posture, the way she fidgeted with her hands—but she soldiered on, even allowing a few handshakes despite her reluctance. Seeing the path I followed, LaDonna took a seat at what would be the head of the room if it had one.

Once we made the rounds, Hanna waved us over to the only booth in the shop—A small circular table in a corner backed with an almost miniature L-shaped padded seat. It was positioned near two wide arched walls, one leading to the larger merchandise room, the other to a hall leading to a second staircase. LaDonna sat on the opposite side of the room in a perfect position to watch the three of us.

Well done, ladies.

"Come on," I coaxed Betony, "I want to talk about witchy shit." That was what Betony always called it when she wanted a tutoring session.

Her steps may have been small, but I suspect the coven's presence around her gave her the impression of inclusion. It was perfect. I could draw her out, and she'd see it as an interview instead of an interrogation.

I sat on one end of the booth, and Betony took the other, placing Hanna between us in the corner. I set my half-empty mug on the table and turned my attention to Betony.

"Have you given any consideration to what kind of witch you are?"

"I have," she said. "I think I might be an orange, like Conall. I tried reading cards for some of the people in my server, and apparently, I did an amazing job." She rolled her eyes. "I hate orange, though. The color, I mean."

I willed my heart to calm down and my thoughts to settle, and found myself thankful for the familiar presence of the coven, even if they made me a little nervous. I needed to discuss her true nature with her without upsetting her, and doing so with the coven here would be so much easier for both of us.

"Betony… I've never told you my history, have I?"

She shook her head, and her pink hair flopped back and forth in front of her eyes. "Hm-mm."

I began the story. Starting from my childhood and asking Hanna to fill in the many places where my memory had holes, I explained how I had grown up with my mother in the arms of the coven. I told her about the night that Hanna, Conall, and I had lost our mothers to a killer who'd never been caught. I explained that after that, I was a quiet kid who, within a short time, began displaying signs of being the gray.

"Do you think your mother's death had anything to do with you being the gray?"

I shook my head, and my crown wiggled. I pulled the bobby pins out and placed the silver monstrosity on the table. "No. We are who we are when we are born—like eye color or height. And that's something I need to explain to you as well, Betony. I recently learned that I'm not the gray."

"What do you mean?" she asked, her expression guarded.

It's like she's afraid to hear what I'm about to say.

"Betony, it took me a while to unravel what happened and why my power went pear-shaped when it did. It changed because sixteen years ago, another fiercely powerful witch came to Gryphon."

"What are you saying?" she asked tremulously, fear in the back of her hazel eyes.

Goddess, I hate to do this to her. I longed to reach out and give her a reassuring touch, but it wouldn't help soften the blow.

"Betony, you're the gray."

Three sets of footsteps drew my eyes across the room. Jake and Cadence stood on either side of a newcomer who I'd never seen outside of online pictures before, but her arrival couldn't have been poorer. Short red hair in a boy cut, clad in denim jeans and a flannel shirt, her stance wasn't aggressive, but it bordered on it.

"Amber," Betony whispered. Guess she hadn't caught wind in the chats.

Of course, she'd show up now. Dammit!

The room grew charged, and conversation dwindled as the two young women locked eyes. Before anyone said another word, Betony jumped from her seat and dashed through the archway from the room, her footsteps pounding up the stairs.

Chapter 23

From Amber's abashed expression and shaking chin, I gathered this was not the reception she'd hoped for. She and I both watched as Rolf, Cadence, and Jake followed Betony. I debated following, but decided it was better to let her handle what I suspect she'd known on some level for a while now—that Betony still felt sensitive where she was concerned. My veranda and coffee shop had hosted many of what the kids jokingly referred to as "prayer meetings;" now my upstairs would as well. With Conall in his furry form present to hear everything said and Cadence and Jake there to reassure her, I was confident she would calm down relatively soon. With what I'd learned about Betony and her hand at turning events in her favor, she'd soon be downstairs with a million questions about what it meant to be a gray and asking how on earth had she not figured it out herself?

I stepped toward Amber cautiously. She looked like a frightened deer about to dart away, and I didn't want her to leave after we'd worked so hard to coax her here.

"I'm sorry," I said earnestly. My hand reached out but pulled back without touching. I didn't know if she shared Betony's dislike of physical contact. "Are you OK?"

It felt like such a ridiculous question, given the circumstances. She nodded, but she was shaking. "I didn't mean to hurt her. I really didn't."

It was the first time I'd heard Amber's beautiful voice. Low for a young woman and a bit gravelly, it reminded me of what LaDonna might have sounded like at seventeen.

"Can… can I go upstairs?"

Eyeing the stairwell, I pursed my lips. "Mmmm, maybe give her some space for a few minutes. Let her chew on the news she just got. We were having a pretty heavy-duty talk before you got here. Not about you," I said, adding the last bit in a rush, in case she misunderstood.

"OK."

"Do you want some food? Or soda?"

She declined, which didn't surprise me, and I said she could stick around as long as she needed to. She gave me a small, grateful smile and wandered self-consciously into the group of coven members.

I had barely had time to feel awkward about not knowing what to do next when a shiver crawled over my entire body and set my teeth on edge. A terrible wrongness crept over me, a sensation foreign within the walls of Blackwell Manor. Thunderous footsteps descended the back staircase to the kitchen, and the back door from the kitchen to the porch slammed. As I stepped that way to see what was going on, Cadence burst into the room.

"Mama Murph, Betony left," she said breathlessly. "She-she took something from your—" she eyed the crowd and decided it didn't matter what she let spill, "from your power room. A book, I think. And she stole the keys to Jake's car. He's outside. I think he's calling 9-1-1."

I reached toward her and grasped her forearms. "Calm down, Cadence. It's all—"

"She took your dog, Mama Murph! *She fucking stole Rolf!*"

Aw, fuck.

The chaos trigger had worked. Now, we needed to decide where to go from here.

☽○☾

What do you do when an unlicensed teenager steals a book from your spell collection and, more than that, absconds with your boyfriend in his furry form, sure that he is her familiar?

You go to your coven, of course, and recruit teenagers and their knowledge of technology.

The frenetic energy triggered by Cadence's dramatic and terrified entrance was still lingering in the room, and I imagined myself soaking in the strength of it like a sea sponge. Soon, my ears were ringing, and my skin felt alive. The space and depth of objects around me grew distinct. Without even trying, I had tapped Source power.

I sent Cadence out to the driveway to stop Jake before he could call 9-1-1. Betony had a rudimentary grasp of driving skills from navigating the vehicles teens in rural Alabama had often driven before—4-wheelers, golf carts, riding mowers—as well as having practiced with her sister a few times. As long as she safely made it out of town, which was only a handful of blocks away, the rest of the nearby streets were backwoods country roads. Still, I asked LaDonna and the rest of the coven to cast a protection spell for her and anyone in her path. No sense allowing a gray witch to stir up more trouble than necessary, especially since her chaos had undoubtedly just been triggered. Based on what I gauged Betony's power to be, it'd take the entire coven to keep her and the world around her safe.

I turned my attention to Jake and Cadence. "Does she have Pingion on her phone?" they nodded in unison. "Can you track her for me?"

Without saying a word, they both whipped out their phones and started typing, their thumbs a blur. I climbed the staircase, and their footsteps were right behind mine, never misjudging a rise as they clicked and beeped. At the top of the stairs, I picked up speed across the short hall into the room that I'd specifically told Betony not to enter again without me. With barely a tug on the Source, I saw the hole on the shelf where the book Betony had taken had been. *Hexes and Jinxes.* The same book she'd asked about reading only days before. I should have known.

I pounded back downstairs as I started considering my alternatives. Driving to her house was a possibility, but there was no certainty that she was headed there. Not to mention that Betony had hinted several times how embarrassed she was about both her home and her parents. I'd only seen the outside a couple of times from driving her home when a ride she'd planned on didn't pan out. If I showed up there, it'd only worsen her frustration and humiliation and augment the chaos she already wielded.

I could use Source power to track her down, but what would that solve? It'd lead to a confrontation when she was clearly in a heated mood and needed to sort through her feelings. What I needed was to get a bead on her mood, so that when she'd calmed down, I could approach her safely without things blowing up. Literally.

I pressed my eyes with the heels of my palms. A hormonal gray witch on a tear had kidnapped Conall when he was shorter than my knee was tall. *Mother Goddess and Father God, please keep him safe. Please.*

"Pingion isn't working. She must have turned her phone off. Do you want me to go after them?" Jake offered. I dropped my hands, and my heart broke at the concern I saw in his downturned eyes.

"You don't have your car," Cadence chided.

He motioned at me in with dramatic swings of his hands in explanation. "I—she has one. I could—"

Noticing that LaDonna and the others had already finished their protection spell, I held up a hand. "That won't be necessary. LaDonna?"

My high priestess turned her attention to me, and I envied her serenity. If she was stressed at all, it didn't reflect on her ageless face. "What can I do, Murphy?"

I licked my lips nervously. "Can you… all of you… help me to astral project and find them?

LaDonna's smile was both reassuring and a little scary. "We sure can."

Chapter 24

Luke, LaDonna's significant other, came to my aid as soon as he heard the plan. My large rolled-arm sofa was pulled away from the wall, and a space cleared for me to lie down. As the coven gathered around, I felt incredibly self-conscious, reclining onto a throw pillow with a black cat on it and swinging my feet up onto the cushion. I wondered how in the hell I could expect to astral project with everyone around me.

Luke pulled up a three-legged stool from the corner near the umbrella stand and sat at my side. "They aren't there," he said soothingly. "Remember that. They are with you, but they aren't there. Everything you need is within. Now close your eyes."

His voice made some part of my lizard brain accept his words as true, and damned if a wave of calm didn't immediately settle over me as I obediently closed my eyes. Conall had a golden voice that I adored, but Luke had a deep, reassuring timbre and a lifetime of experience as a witch, many as second-in-command of a coven. His words had authority but without being authoritative. It spoke to my soul.

"Breathe in, Murphy. Feel your lungs filling and your ribs touching your arms as your body melts into the couch beneath you."

His words pattered on like soft rain, and soon it became my whole world. My body sagged into the cushions under me as my muscles softened and my mind mellowed. Colors swirled behind my eyelids, and my breathing grew steady and deep. When he suggested I let go of my physical form, it seemed like the most natural act in the world.

Just let go. Just let it go.

I noticed myself *above* myself and saw the coven in a circle, with their hands joined. They had included Cadence, Jake, and Amber in the ritual, and I loved them even more for it. Luke was still positioned near me, his voice coaching my spirit.

"And now, Murphy, I want you to imagine Conall and Betony. Allow your senses to reach out beyond the walls and into the astral body of knowledge. See the streets below, the trees, the homes. Allow them to draw you like a magnet."

I had left the four walls of my home, and I hadn't even been aware of it happening. It felt as if my spirit was meant to coast on the information current coursing through the universe. Roads, cars, homes, and businesses passed beneath me as I flew, unaware of cold or wind, space or time. I was a part of everything, and it was a part of me. My body was the equivalent of a tiny atom in the macrocosm of the universe.

Conall... Betony... Conall... Betony...

I had no sense of time. Somehow, eternity and a moment had both had passed when I saw Jake's sports car, an old, white Mitsubishi fixer-upper that he was incredibly proud of, parked below me. Around it were a couple of broken-down sheds and a crumbling house with cinderblock steps. Two old trucks flanked Jake's car, which looked like Betony had parked it diagonally in a hurry.

Any stress or panic I felt had vanished; only a sense of purpose harmonized with a feeling of unity remained in me.

I moved from above the roof through it, drawn to my purpose below. Soon, I was surrounded by off-white walls draped with pride flags and Hot Topic décor. Betony sat on the floor, legs in a V, her black and white clown face paint streaked with tears. Before her stood a Mason jar filled with various items. Rusty nails. Vinegar. Dog feces. Milk. Lemon. Plastic containers of onion and chili powders lay on the floor near the book she'd stolen from my library.

Never a good idea to start a spell with an unethical act, my dear.

I blinked.

Blinked?

And realized I saw the world from about eighteen inches high. And was breathing. And damn, everything smelled so *strong!*

Murphy?

Yep. I'd once again dropped into Conall's body. Only this time, he was Rolf.

☽○☾

Murphy? It was odd, having a mental conversation within the same mind, but Conall and I had done it before.

Yes, it's me.

But how?

My spirit lifted the way it does when I smile. *Luke.*

If Rolf's little doggie self could chuckle, it would have. **Of course**.

Although the lid to the Mason jar was closed, the contents of Betony's sour jar were nearly overwhelming my—Conall's—canine olfactory sense. Poor Conall had to suffer through her assembling all the contents. The thought made me shudder, and Conall raised off his haunches and shook to disguise my reaction before panting and walking to Betony and nosing her on the arm.

"Hey, Rolf," she crooned. "I know all this is new for you, but you'll be OK. I'll talk to Murphy and bring her book back when all of this is done, and I'll help her understand. You belong here with me. You get me, don't you, buddy?"

"Rolf" sat back down and tilted our head to study her, and I felt Conall's attempt to make his face seem concerned. She reached over and sought reassurance by ruffling "her familiar's" head before turning her attention back to her spell. She consulted the book a moment before taking a candle and a plastic lighter from her collection of spelling material.

It was time for her to seal the jar and complete the ritual. As one, Conall and I stood and braced ourselves to pull her arm away from her sour jar. Surely, if the animal she viewed as her familiar stopped her before she sealed the spell, she'd take that as a clue it wasn't wise.

She flicked the lighter, which glowed brightly against her dark nail polish. The sound of a slamming door caused a flicker of her eyes toward her bedroom door, but intent as she was on completing her spell, it distracted her only a moment. We stepped toward Betony, who eyed us for a second before moving the lighter to the wick. Our oddly long dog jaw opened to grip her arm as the door to Betony's room flew open.

A rangy man with deep-set wrinkles and small, darting eyes stood in the doorway. With him wafted the odor of smoked cigarettes and marijuana. Betony, startled, lost her grip on the lighter and nearly toppled the jar as her legs jerked inward and took on a defensive stance.

"Dad! You can't do that! You should knock first!" Anger and alarm made her voice shake, and her eyes darted to the ingredients. In the sweat coming from her body, I sensed a sudden rise in tension, fear, and apprehension.

The man scoffed, his breath foul from lack of dental hygiene. "S'my damn house. I'll walk into whatever fuckin' room I want whenever I damn well please." His eyes met ours. "Why do you got a goddamn dog?"

Betony's jaw clenched for only the briefest moment before she forced herself to relax. I smelled a fast rise in her perspiration levels. And anxiety. Interesting. I'd never known what it smelled like before. It was tart, but with oomph.

"It's… Murphy's. My friend from the coffee shop."

"Well, you better damn well bring that fucker back to her ASAP. We got enough critters around here to feed. We don't need ano—"

His beady eyes darted around the items Betony had gathered around her, and his eyes grew large.

He understood. Even high, he recognized a sour jar when he saw one. *Well, I'll be damned.*

"Girl, what the fuck you doin'?" His hand made a white-knuckled fist on the doorknob, as if he saw it as a neck to throttle.

Her mouth flapped. She hadn't expected to be caught, and it's hard to explain away a jar full of vinegar and dog shit. "I... um..."

"You're making a goddamn sour jar, ain't you?"

Betony's eyes widened. "How do you—?"

Betony's father stormed into the room and loomed over her, and she raised her arms protectively and turned her face away. Plainly, it wasn't the first time she'd felt physically threatened. A low growl rose in my throat.

"Goddamn it, girl. What the fuck is wrong wichyou? Your momma and I raised you better'n that. Dragged you into church'n' everythin'. We was trying to get away from all that shit! You ain't gonna be no witch. Them cunning folk ain't nothing but trouble." His fists were balled near the hips of his dirty jeans, and he radiated anger like heat. My muscles grew taut as Conall and I prepared to launch at him in any available tender spot if need be.

Betony dropped her arms, and her mouth flapped a few times before she stammered, "How did you—?"

He pointed a finger at her and somehow made the act violent. "You was supposed to be special. Didja know that?"

Supposed to be?

"Your momma and I, we tried to make sure you was when you was a baby. Make you the best of all of 'em. Make you the Summit. We took out three of 'em in the middle of an monolith ritual before we had to run. They almost got us, but they never did. Even taking all of that power away from 'em, it didn't change nothin.' You still a goddamn nothing."

Monolith ritual?

I think he means megalith ritual. It's one our coven used to do. I don't know much about it—Dad's never talked about it. The last time they did, it was the night our mothers died.

Betony's posture grew tall, and her uneasy brow grew flat over a pair of stormy eyes. She pushed herself up to standing, and the small child grew into a woman who nearly matched her father in height and weight.

"You. Knew." Her voice carried the calm only heard in the darkest of rage, and her body appeared to be smoking—no, not smoking. And it wasn't her body. Her aura had embraced what she now fully recognized. Betony exuded her aura in her power, which now wafted off her in tendrils of smoke—the gray.

I smelled her father's sour fear now, but he did his best to uphold his façade of control. "'Course we knew. We ain't stupid."

"You told me I had to go to church! You told me witches were evil! That they were from the devil!"

"Witches ain't any good, Bet! Our family got cunnin' folk runnin' back for years, but it ain't never done us any good, now has it? Your life been great? You like living in this shitty house?"

Betony's fists matched her father's now, balled at her hips, and her neck jutted forward as she got into his face. "If you'd just keep a *job*—"

He raised a hand, and Betony flinched, expecting the blow that never came. He dropped his hand, despondent. "I'm a fucking criminal, Bet. You know how hard it is to get a good job when you got a record?"

Betony's chest rose and fell in deep breaths with forced control. When she spoke, the low, measured, clipped voice barely sounded like her.

"Well, maybe you aren't the only criminal in the family."

Betony turned and extended her arm toward her dresser, where a large pair of scissors lay. The blades leaped off and flew several feet into her hand, handle first. For the merest fraction of a second, her face reflected shock. Then, with a slight uptick on one side of her mouth, she pivoted back to face her father and stabbed him forcefully under his ribs.

I had no time to respond. Her father's eyes bulged, and his hands wrapped around hers, covered in rivulets of blood. His shocked eyes met her furious ones, and I noticed with heartbreak that they were the same beautiful shade of hazel. He fell forward and gripped the edge of her bed, knocking over her sour jar and kicking the stolen book, spilling his life-giving fluid onto its open pages. She swept his feet out from under him and watched without pity as he fell.

"Where there's a witch, there's a way, bitch," she said sharply before reaching down and scooping me—us—up in her arms. I fought furiously, kicking my muscular hind legs desperately so I could stay and see if we could help her father, but she gripped us tighter to her chest until we could barely breathe. She nabbed her purse from where it hung from a post of her brass bed and dashed for the door.

Chapter 25

Her father.

I know.

Do you think he's dead?

Betony threw open the door to Jake's car and tossed us in, not giving us a chance to turn around and escape before the door slammed in our face.

I couldn't tell. Stomach wounds can take a while to kill, I've heard.

Betony stalked around the front of the car, yanked open the driver's side door, and squeezed into the driver's seat with barely a look at us. She threw her purse into the small backseat before cranking the ignition with a blood-soaked hand, yanking the car into reverse, and spinning the Eclipse into a half-circle before throwing gravel in her wake as she flew from the driveway. I watched the landscape race by as Betony drove. I wasn't sure where she was headed; she'd steered the car down unfamiliar roads.

After a few moments of weaving down the road, Betony seemed a bit more composed, and her trembling subsided. Her expression revealed little about what she was thinking other than the odd way her mouth pulled thoughtfully at the corners.

"Want some fresh air, boy?" Betony asked, her voice bland with forced control. Her fingers found the window button and levered it down.

As the window cracked at the top, I stood on my hind legs to better smell the surrounding air. My paws clawed the plastic window ledge, and my short hind legs wavered like a new sailor's as I tried to find balance during Betony's erratic, inexperienced drive. I raised my nose to the air rushing inside, and when we hit a bump in the road, I allowed my spirit to dislodge. A tipsy sense of vertigo washed over me as I rose above the car roof and beyond, watching as the Eclipse flew down the road below.

Yes, Conall was in a car with Betony, but he was also a witch capable of becoming human again if he needed to gain control of a problem. Betony's father, however, lay bleeding in his house with a pair of scissors lodged in his gut. I needed to go back to my body.

I allowed myself to be conscious of the journey back to my body, but as I skimmed the tops of the trees, I never stopped thinking. Where was Betony heading? Did she regret what she'd done? Had it been a moment of passion, or was it something she'd wanted to do for a while? What would become of her? And did I care what happened to the man who killed my mother, and Hanna's and Conall's? Did he deserve to live?

The fields became familiar roads. I passed the water tower, the post office, the small clump of businesses. Eventually, I coasted across Oberon Street and through the recognizable walls of my shop and to the sofa where my body lay reclining, looking as peaceful as I wished I felt.

The drone of Luke's voice tapered off as he sensed my return, and he allowed me a moment to collect myself as I reoriented my spirit within my body. My eyes fluttered open, and I saw his crooked grin and thick, dark beard bent up into a welcome smile below his bald head. I noticed that Amber, Jake and Cadence had left the circle, and I wondered where they had gone, and when.

"Y'allright, love?" Luke leaned forward a bit, but avoided touching me. I recognized at that moment that one reason I understood Betony's dislike of being touched was that I had the same reluctance. Luke, being the wise soul that he was, recognized and respected my space.

"I'm OK. But…" I noticed Amber watching from the archway, her hauntingly beautiful rust-colored eyes overwhelmed with concern.

"Amber," I said, raising my head, "Can you find Jake and Cadence for me?" She licked her lips and reluctantly agreed, but I sensed from the way she dragged her feet as she left the room that she hated not knowing what I was about to say. I paused until she was out of earshot and allowed my head to flop back onto the pillow. "Betony… and Conall. They're not OK."

I hurriedly explained the events of the last few minutes, culminating with the need to get help for Betony's father. Yes, he may be a murderer, but allowing him to bleed and die was something a person like him would do—not a person like me. He could face justice another way.

"Do you know the address?" LaDonna asked.

"No. It's a trailer on Old Harper Road with a couple of old sheds and two trucks parked in front—one red, one white. Cinderblock steps. It's on the…." I paused, my brain still awhirl in the turbulence and disorientation, "North side of the road. Huge tree in the front yard. And a dog tied to a zipline." Knowing I'd sadly just described a significant portion of the homes on Old Harper Road, my shoulders melted with despair. Undeterred, Miriam pulled a cell phone from a Renaissance tailcoat pocket of her steampunk costume and dialed the police. Her soft-soled boots barely made a sound as she explained to the emergency operator there was a situation on Old Harper Road. Her fiercely hairsprayed bleached-blond French twist looked as severe as the tone in her voice.

Cadence and Jake returned with Amber close behind. I asked them if they knew Betony's house number and got nothing but head shakes in return.

LaDonna approached me with an iced glass of what I recognized to be peppermint tea from my refrigerator. I slowly sat up and took it, thankful that I kept it handy; it would quickly ease my fluttering stomach and fatigue. I took a long swallow, and the mint cooled my throat and made it easier to breathe.

The sound of a phone alert pinging in Cadence's pocket made us all turn. Her blue eyes grew, and she removed it from her pocket, unlocking it with practiced ease. Her eyes panned the screen, and she looked up with panic painted on her face.

"It's the Pingion app. Betony's—"

The sound of Jake's after-market muffler rumbling in the driveway told us what Cadence hadn't had time to say. Betony had returned.

Chapter 26

I headed toward the archway at the edge of the room with my mind reeling. What would I say when she came in? Was she here for help? To ask us to help her turn herself in? To yell at us for telling her she was the gray, maybe accuse us of lying or hiding something from her?

I felt a gentle pressure on the back of my hand and looked down to see LaDonna's fingertips touching me. She lifted her eyes to mine, and I saw peace, calm, and wisdom in them. In a flash, I recalled the last meeting back in her home, and the coven holding hands in a circle as the power of the Source coursed through me into Conall, Hanna, and the rest of the coven. I remembered how my feet felt connected through the wood in her floors beneath me to the Source that touched us all.

I remembered my power.

I kicked off my shoes and wiggled my toes on the cherry wood planks of my home. In my mind, I imagined the sun that provided energy to the wood from a seed, the water that had helped it grow, the earth that had provided the nutrients, and the sun that had helped it photosynthesize. I saw the sweat of the person who felled the tree, the next who shaped the planks, the spirit and vision of the architect who'd created the home I lived in, and the love and memories imbued amidst the walls of the building that had housed my mother and me for the first ten years of my life and now supplied my revenue.

It was all connected. *We* were all connected.

Footsteps on the porch told me she was coming in through the kitchen, and the sound of doggie claws on the tile followed the creak and slam of the screen and the interior doors. The faucet ran, and I suspected that Betony was trying to rinse the worst of the blood from her hands. No one said a word. The room stood in silence like antelopes who had heard the swish of a lion walking through tall grass as we waited for Betony. The energy in the room shimmered like summer heat.

Rolf strode into the parlor room and headed straight for me, butting my leg with his furry head concernedly. I bent down and gave him a soothing scratch under the chin and around his pointed ears. Rex emerged from his hiding place under the couch and wound himself around the small dog, his tail erect, and his ears alert.

Betony straggled into the room where we stood facing the portal as she strode through. Blood splatter stained the tops of her thick-soled boots and the cuffs of her hoodie. She'd slung her backpack over one shoulder, almost like an afterthought. She saw everyone in the room stopped to take in her arrival, and her eyes grew large, settled on me, and eased like a soldier arriving home from war.

"Mama Murph..." Tears fell from her eyes, streaking through what was left of the caked black face paint and leaving trails of gray through the white. Words wouldn't come from her or anyone else who empathized with her pain. I felt my throat thicken, looking at the agony on her face.

Maybe I was a fool, or sentimental, or blind, but when I saw the genuine heartbreak on Betony's face, my arms reached out, and she ran to them. I wrapped my arms around her, awkwardly navigating my left hand under her backpack, and for once, Betony was okay with human contact. Her body shook with sobs, and I stroked her pink hair.

"Shhh, Bet. It will be OK." I didn't know if it would be OK at all. I'd had no experience with this, but I had to ease her pain somehow.

"Murphy, my dad. I-I-"

"I know."

She pulled back with a startled jerk and met my steady gaze. Snot ran from her nose, and she wiped it unceremoniously on the sleeve of her hoodie without an inkling of self-consciousness. Luke approached her with a fistful of tissues he must have scavenged from my downstairs bathroom, and she accepted them gratefully and wiped her face. From the corner of my eye, I saw Rolf darting from the room to the kitchen.

"You." Her voice shuddered, and she sucked in a coughing sob before trying again. "You do?"

Betony had always given me credit for having more power than I knew I had, but today, she was correct. Perhaps she had sensed it all along. "I was there," I admitted.

Her mouth opened, and her expression wavered between impressed, baffled, and appalled. When she finally found her voice, she said, "How?"

"I astral projected."

"Gray witches can do that?"

I paused and realized that I'd never had a chance to explain to Betony that I wasn't a gray before she'd run off. I'd told her part of the story, but in the commotion, some facts probably got jumbled.

"I don't know," I admitted. "I'm not a gray. I thought I was, but that's you, and I'm something else."

Betony swallowed and hiccupped back a sob. "If you're not a gray, are you some other type?"

I sensed she had a clue, but I didn't want to say. From the way her father had ranted on about an appointing ceremony and, as he put it, a "Summit," she might have a negative impression of what it meant to be a Summate. I decided to dial down the description for now.

"I'm a little all of them, I think. I'm still trying to figure that out. I just learned it myself."

Betony stepped back, evaluating me from the top of my Halloween extra red-dyed hair to the hem of my ridiculously flared-out Glinda dress with its many petticoats. Her brow furrowed and her eyes flashed.

"Are you the Summit?"

I paused and considered my words for a moment. She'd just heard from her father that he felt the Summate was "the best of all of 'em." Would she hate me for being the witch her father had wanted her to be?

"That's what we think. I've displayed several different skills, which is unusual unless I'm the Summate."

"You're the Summate." She scoffed, her misery forgotten in a flood of confusion and frustration. "My dad wanted me to be the Summate." It was impossible to read her tone. She kicked at nothing on the floor and dropped her attention to the tops of her bloodstained boots.

"I heard that," I said softly. "I also heard that he and your mother killed my mother, and Hanna's, and Conall's."

Immediately, her body became a live wire, charged with energy and jumpy with power. "Is that *my* fault?" she barked. "I was a fucking baby!"

I held a hand out placatingly. "No, Betony. That's not what I—"

"I had no way to control what he did then or what he did when he raised me and hurt me and my mom. I've never had control of anything in my life, and now you're telling me I'm the gray, some chaos witch. I'll bet that means you think I'm going to live closed off and alone, the way you do, for the rest of my life. I am *not* going to live like that. I *can't* live alone like that, Murphy! I can't!"

The idea of living an isolated life was appalling to Betony, who lived for her friends and her social media and her outings.

"I'm not alone anymore, Betony," I replied. "I have my friends and my coven. It doesn't have to be that way for you if you don't want it to be. Let us help you, Betony. We can try to figure out how to work with it."

"Like they helped you? They didn't do *shit* for you. No, thank you!"

Her eyes darted around in panicked haste in search of something. "Where's Rolf?"

I swallowed and panned the floor, looking for the dog. "Rolf" was nowhere to be found, and I wasn't sure where he'd gone. A rustling on the veranda side of the house drew everyone's attention to the place where Conall entered with a small cluster of the coven on either side of him, looking more abashed than I'd ever seen.

"Where's Rolf?" Betony repeated, her panic level rising. I stepped forward, aching to lay a hand on her arm to ease her tension but refraining, knowing that it would only worsen it.

"Rolf isn't your dog, Betony."

"*Where is Rolf?*"

"Right here," Conall said, his hands protectively over his middle as if he was still undressed and expected a blow to his groin for his honesty.

Betony froze, and I could almost hear the wheels in her head registering this new piece of information. "You were a dog." Her voice was cold, lacking emotion. Conall nodded. She let out a short, incredulous snort from her nose. "That's why you were following me around. Not because you liked me. Fuck. Nothing in my life is what I thought it was. Nothing."

It struck me as bizarre that she gave the same weight to Rolf being her familiar as she did to her mother and father killing the mothers of three people whose lives she claimed to value, but I also hadn't lived her life.

"I was the dog," Conall admitted.

Betony scoffed and studied the tops of her boots, seeming to see the blood droplets for the first time.

"How?" Her voice was biting, angry, bitter. "You're an orange witch."

Conall delivered his disarming smile, but it didn't affect Betony, who remained stone-faced. "A spell," he admitted. "LaDonna has power over both flora and fauna, being a green witch. She cast it."

Betony's gaze shot back and forth from Conall to me, ignoring anyone else in the room. "Why?"

"We wanted to keep you safe," I said. "You and everyone around you. We didn't know for sure at first."

"That I was the gray?"

I nodded. "I suspected," I admitted. "But I thought it might still be me. Until we knew for sure, we thought it best if Conall kept an eye on you. His prophecy skills might have helped him to see danger coming."

Betony nodded in tandem, then broke her rhythm and started shaking her head instead. "Y'all are unbelievable. Everyone wants to control me. My parents. My friends. You two."

"It wasn't about control—"

"*Then what was it about?*" Her voice wasn't a shriek, but it was close.

"We didn't want you to hurt anyone. Including yourself."

She scoffed again, her composure startlingly back in place, her mind undoubtedly flashing back to the scissors she'd driven into her father's abdomen less than an hour before. "A bit late for that, aren't you?"

She pivoted on the soft rubber sole of her boot, and Jake's voice called out from the back of the room. "Betony!"

Betony whirled back around, eyes flashing. A bulb on a table lamp flashed and popped before it went black, and a startled noise came from behind me as someone grabbed what sounded like a cup sliding across a table.

It's starting.

"*What?*" Betony barked.

"My keys," he said softly. "I need them back."

She sneered and dug into her backpack, where she found Jake's keys. Jake hadn't moved from where he stood, and I wondered if this was a ploy to pull her back into the room where we could contain her. Betony clearly thought so as well.

"Here," she said and hurled them in his direction. I followed the arching path of the keychain with my eyes. Jake lunged forward to catch them, and he dropped them the instant they touched his hand, which came away rusty red with her father's drying blood. Jake made a horrified noise and gripped the wrist of his bloody hand with his opposite palm as if he expected his contaminated hand to become possessed.

When I turned back to where Betony had stood a moment ago, she was gone.

Chapter 27

Betony's absence left an energy vacuum behind as the door closed after her. In my peripheral vision, I noticed a few coven members sinking heavily into seats around the parlor. It was now nine forty-five in the evening. The three remaining teens approached me abashedly and apologized for having to leave to be home before their ten o'clock curfews. They promised to track Betony through Pingion in case I needed help to find her.

On the other side of the room, Miriam still had her ear pressed to her phone. That was a good sign. Maybe 9-1-1 was keeping her on in case they needed us.

"Conall?" He was at my side in a heartbeat. "Will you get the charged water from upstairs? The jar from the last coven meeting?"

He nodded. "Good idea."

I would have gotten it myself, but I wanted to be present in case Miriam needed my input on the call. Sure enough, as Conall returned with the jar and several small glasses, Miriam extended the phone to me so I could offer guidance to the officers en route to Betony's house. When they asked how I knew something was wrong, I lied and said I'd been on the phone with Betony when I'd heard a scuffle. They thought they'd be reporting to a standard domestic call and saw no reason to keep me on the phone when I confirmed they'd found the correct house. I heard the familiar sound of Betony's dog, Rascal, barking through the phone and one officer saying, "Here, again?" as I hit the End button.

I rushed upstairs to change out of my costume, opting instead for my standard jeans and Doc Martens topped with a t-shirt. As I descended the stairs, Hanna came to my side, her face clouded with concern. She'd changed from her Queen of Hearts costume into more serviceable clothes as well—jeans and an oversized sweater. "Should we have kept Betony here?"

I shook my head. "We need to give her a few minutes alone to calm down, or she might go postal. She's got to figure some things out."

"Murphy, she already killed her dad. How much worse could it get?"

"I know, and I don't want her trying to kill anyone else tonight."

She and I helped Conall serve glasses of Source-charged water to the coven. Knowing what I intended to ask them to do next, I knew they'd need a full measure of power to do it. I served LaDonna and Luke first, and as I bent down to give the high priestess her glass, she said, "Shall I bring in the Lughaidh cauldron?"

Amazed, I pulled back, and then I noticed the shy smile on Luke's face. He'd foreseen the need for the clan cauldron, and so they'd brought it. Of course, he did. I nodded, and Luke rose to fetch the coven's favorite tool from their SUV.

As Conall continued to serve the coven, I leaned in to speak with LaDonna in hushed tones.

"Protection spell?" she suggested.

I shook my head. "Binding spell. The strongest one you know. We need to keep Betony from hurting herself or anyone else, and after that, we can focus on protecting the town against her grayness."

LaDonna nodded, and I realized I'd just instructed my high priestess instead of the other way around for the first time.

"Do you have anything of Betony's?"

"There's a small stack of ankle socks behind the register near the sales ledger," I said. She smiled amusedly, but didn't ask why.

I hastened to join Conall in dispensing the water, and when we finished, I motioned to Hanna and Conall to join me in the hall. LaDonna's voice rang through the bottom story. As the three of us rushed through the vestibule to the backdoor and down the veranda steps, she asked the coven members to assemble the requisite materials from the storefront.

I looked at my watch. Ten minutes after ten. Twenty-five minutes had passed since Betony had stormed from the building. She had no car, and lord knew she wouldn't be contacting her mother for a ride anyplace—especially home, where her father was bleeding from a stab wound that she'd inflicted. I wondered how long it would take for an ambulance to arrive now that the cops were on the scene.

My mind reeled as I considered Betony's possible options for places to take refuge. It was Samhain—the veil between the living and the dead was thin, the Walker Hill Cemetery was only two blocks away, and Betony's favorite family member was her deceased grandmother, the one person she knew who loved and accepted her just as she was.

"Walker Hill," I said and started hoofing in that direction. Conall and Hanna hustled after me.

"We're not driving?" Conall asked.

I shook my head. I couldn't explain it, but walking was the way to go. If there was one concept I'd had drilled home in the past few weeks, trusting the Source was always the way to go.

Half a block down the road, my phone pinged, and I pulled it from my back pocket. Amber, it appeared, had formed a new chat group. I kept my feet rushing forward as I read.

Amber Jade: *Betony, are yoi OK?*

Bet: *No I'm not fucking OK. What do you think asshole?*

Two-tone siren song: *Where are you?*

Bet: *I need help. Can y'all help me? I need to focus some power for something.*

Cadence: *You need to turn yourself in.*

Two-tone siren song: *Turn herself in? What happe ed*

Bet: *Cadence it's not your problem. I need help.*

Cadence: *She stabbed her dad.*

Two-tone siren song: *wtf Betony?*

Bet: *You both know how bad he was to my mom and me. Mostly me. At least when he fucked mom she probably wanted it some of the time.*

The implication of her words was so horrific that it took a moment for my mind to register. *Holy shit.* Had the others known? Why hadn't anyone said anything, or gone to the authorities? Or was this the first they'd heard of it as well? As much as Betony had confided in me, I didn't know that about her. I paused for a moment so I could thumb a response:

> Mama Murph: Betony, if that's what's been going on, you have a defense for what you did.

I tried to keep typing, but before I had a chance, a message popped up.

Mama Murph has been removed from the group.

Fuck.

Chapter 28

As I suspected, the lock and chain to Walker Hill Cemetery lay in pieces on the ground. I tried not to think about the height of power Betony had reached to lever enough torque to mangle the thick steel like that.

She'd left the gate open behind her—not smart on Halloween night if she wanted to be alone. Maybe she didn't.

I pushed the creaking, black iron gate open a tiny bit so the three of us could enter the cemetery astride one another. Walker Hill encompassed nearly eighty acres of graves and low, rolling hills; Betony could be anywhere—if she was here at all. I felt a pull northward and followed it up the gravel road like a bloodhound tracking a scent. Conall and Hanna trailed me closely, as silent as specters.

As we crested a short rise, I saw her: Betony, still in her clown costume, now rumpled and hanging from her frame. She had a new board on the grave before her; the plastic shrink wrap lay discarded in a pile on the grave beside her. I saw in the glint of moonlight the familiar circle planchette from a newly unwrapped Mystic Spiral game.

I motioned to Conall and Hanna to duck behind a nearby mausoleum. Perhaps if Betony could speak to her grandmother, she might hear a soothing voice she needed. It was worth giving her a chance.

We were barely close enough to hear Betony's voice, which had shrunk from its normal, boisterous level in her sadness.

Her fingers poised on the planchette, Betony called. "Gramma? Are you here? I need help. Please."

I tapped into a deeper intensity of Source power. Across the cemetery, a handful of ghostly forms glowed and meandered among the gravestones, and they seemed content where they were. None of them stood near Betony.

"Gramma?" Betony's voice broke, and she sobbed, her body hunched over in grief and despair.

A silvery hand emerged from within the grave below, followed by the rest of an ethereal body.

Oh, thank goodness.

The silver hand touched the planchette and moved it, probably to the word *Hello*. That was standard.

"Gramma?" Her voice choked with joy now, and Betony sat up to better help her relative move the piece so they could converse.

Without warning, a glowing, sickly, yellow-orange, undulating, misshapen form emerged from a cloud that came from nowhere. The shape was rangy, and I caught the odor of sulfur mixed with marijuana and cigarettes on the next breeze.

Betony's father's physical body had died, but his aggrieved energy had found her, and he wasn't there to plead for her forgiveness. I emerged from behind the mausoleum, and my hand raised to get Betony's attention. My mouth opened to cry out a warning, but the sickly form slid into the planchette in a sulfurous lightning bolt, traveled up Betony's fingers into her arm, her body, and filled her form.

Rage filled me. He'd found yet another way to invade and violate Betony. Now, not only did I have to deal with Betony and her uncontrolled, untrained chaos energy, I had to contend with the dark, confused soul of an evil dead man.

Aw, fuck!

I retreated behind the mausoleum again to gather my thoughts, positioning myself to monitor Betony, who was trying to speak to her grandmother without success. Her poor grandma was struggling in vain to wrench the offensive ghost from within her granddaughter. Betony must have sensed her grandma's touch; she pulled her hoodie around her tightly and rocked back and forth.

"What's wrong?" Hanna whispered.

In hushed tones, I told them what I'd learned from the group chat on my way to the cemetery and finished the story with the battle invisible to them that was happening on the hill before us. The appalled looks on their faces matched the disgust I'd felt as the story unraveled.

"Can we fight her? Them?" Conall asked.

I shook my head. "I'm an untrained Summate, and she's an untrained gray and possessed besides. I have no idea how to handle this."

"She has otherworldly strength," Hanna observed. "Maybe we need otherworldly strength, too."

Of course! And with the veil between the living and the dead so weak, there's no better night to ask.

Reading her mind, the way we so often did, Conall led the three of us through the dark and trees to the other side of the cemetery and the plot of land where our mothers lay in neighboring graves.

We joined hands near the foot of their plot. It was up to me; Conall and Hanna didn't have the power to call the dead without a tool like a Ouija board or a Mystic Spiral; only I had the power of black witches.

My heart hammered, and I knew they felt the way my fingers trembled in their hands. Normally, I tried to cast in rhyme because I appreciated the pattern and rhythm, and it helped my energy, but there was no time to linger on niceties or drum up fancy words just for effect. Lifting my face to the sky, I found the waxing crescent moon overhead in a wide break in the clouds and used it as a focus object as I spoke:

> "Hermes, Mercury, Ankou, Persephone,
> Guardians of the gates and guides to the spirits of our ancestors,
> We ask you to call our mothers, Nora Blackwell, Leah Chava, and Veronica Barry,
> We, the bone of their bone and blood of their blood,
> desire their assistance, their guidance,
> their knowledge, and their protection.
> The Samhain veil is thin
> Please let our loved ones in."

The pattern of the final few words resonated with me, and I repeated it. Conall and Hanna joined me, and as the spell's power grew in strength, a light rain began. I closed my eyes and bathed in the rhythm of the words, the chill in the falling water, in the closeness of my two best friends, and in the love and power we channeled between us. I imagined an otherworldly curtain pulled back by ghostly hands.

The call of a crow perched in a tree behind me told me we'd succeeded, and the energy in the air around us shifted and became charged. I opened my eyes. Beside us stood three wavering, orbital forms that oscillated between a glowing silvery-white and rose. The raindrops reflected the brilliant colors as they swept past.

"They're here," I breathed, and then I realized that my friends' eyes flickered with the same silvery-rose color as the orbs.

"You can see them, too!" I cried. Their eyes both appeared glassy with wonder and joy.

"See who?"

Crap. Betony had found us. That she couldn't see the positive energy that made up the ghosts around us told me everything I needed to know about the place where her mind had gone.

"We're visiting with our mothers," I tried to keep my tone as matter-of-fact as possible, but Betony, filled with her father's rage and the chaotic energy she harnessed naturally, saw an opportunity to argue.

"You mean the ones my mom and dad killed?" Her voice was acid.

I tried to think of a way to appease her, but words refused to come. My thoughts felt ensnared like a dolphin in a net.

She managed to fuck up your life without being near you, Murphy. How well do you think you're going to handle her chaos when she's standing fifteen feet away and wants to use it?

The bright orbs circled us and placed themselves protectively between Betony and us. Fueled by their presence, I stood taller and faced the young woman who had, until tonight, viewed me as a mentor.

"Betony, your father has passed away," I told her. "You killed him."

She swallowed, and a split second of panic washed over her pale face, but what came out was a shaky, "Good."

"I know, because," I paused. There was no way she'd take this well, but it had to be said. "His spirit invaded you a few minutes ago when you were on your grandmother's grave."

"No." The word was a denial, and she stepped away as if I held a cattle prod aimed in her direction. "No. No way. My Gramma was there, and she would never let him do that. It was my grandmother. My Gramma's with me."

"She tried to fight him and couldn't," I explained. "You felt cold when you sat there, didn't you? On your upper arm?"

"He's not in me!" I felt the pain and torment in those four words that reflected a lifetime of denial, and my heart ached for her.

The ground trembled beneath my feet, and I stepped away, grabbing Conall and Hanna and pulling them with me as I did. Nearby headstones tipped and toppled as the rain-dampened ground surrounding them rippled and broke. Fall flowers and other grave decorations took flight like blind birds, colliding with each other and sending petals and debris raining over the fallen grave markers.

"He's not in me!" Betony raged, and the heavy headstones cracked and lifted and swirled with the lighter wreckage. The orbs moved to cover us like spiritual umbrellas and blocked the falling rubble. My friends and I continued to back away, our eyes never leaving Betony's face. Her once hazel eyes had turned a bright shade of gray and stared at us from under a heavy brow coated with long, wet, pink hair.

"We need the coven," I said, pulling my friends with me as I ran.

Betony followed.

Chapter 29

The two blocks from the cemetery back to my home stretched for an eternity. Betony was not a runner, but fueled by her father's envious, evil, dark drive, her steps never waned. Her breath sounded even and controlled. Fueled by adrenaline and fear, the three of us dashed south and west to Oberon Street, which was slick with rain.

Pop!

A streetlight ahead died in a burst of amber sparks. Then another. *Shit. Betony's getting stronger. She's learning to control it.*

Pop!

I thought of the families inside for the night and hoped the rain would keep them indoors. Mentally, I cast a quick protection spell in their defense.

Mother Goddess, make this right. Protect these families through the night. Let them know they're not alone, but safe and blessed within their home.

A Jack-o-lantern flew in front of us as if thrown by a giant quarterback, and I had to pause, so I didn't collide with it.

"Shit!"

Another streetlight farther down died in a hail of sparks, and as it did, the décor from a house to my right took flight. Orange and purple string lights, black bats, and green-faced witches joined Styrofoam gravestones in a swirling cacophony of obstacles.

I struck out at it and was rewarded with the sharp end of a plastic stake scraping my hand. "Shit!" I repeated, charging through the mess. There was no time to play dodge'em with Halloween decorations.

The orbs that had followed at our side stretched and surrounded us in a glowing wall to protect us from the mess as the list of debris hindering our progress grew. Stretchy spiderwebs, plastic skeletons, and a deflated giant dragon that had once stood in a neighbor's yard all flew around us as if we were in the eye of a tornado meant for us alone.

"Goddamn it!" Conall swore. It was impossible to see past the clutter. We had to keep one foot in front of another and pray that our mothers would guide and shield us.

Wood splintered to my left, and the spiky end of a fence picket broke through the cloud of random flying yard décor and stopped only inches from my eyes. A tricycle found a hole in our protective wall, crossed before us, and joined the swirling mess on the other side. A second fence picket pierced a gap in our shields and stabbed Conall in his abdomen.

He fell to the street, landing hard on his knees. He gripped his side with a groan of pain. From the look of it, the point had entered him at least half a dozen inches deep.

Conall! No!

A sheen of cold sweat covered me as I watched, paralyzed in horror, as blood flowed in a steady current from his wound. Hanna's eyes met mine, equally panicked. Every medical show I'd ever seen came back to me. Don't remove the object impaling him; he could bleed out. Had the picket hit any vital organs? We were less than half a block from my house; could we move him there safely?

If we move him, he could lose too much blood and die. The wood could rip more stuff apart and hurt goddess knows what else inside of him. But we can't stay here, or Betony will be right on us!

I fell to a knee and took Conall's face into my hand. It hadn't taken long for him to grow pale, and a cold sheen of sweat was already forming on his lip and brow. His deep brown eyes met mine with the faith that if there was a way to get him to safety, I would find it. I wished that I shared his conviction.

Loudly popping roots and snapping branches followed by creaks and a thud told me that Betony had uprooted a tree in our path. When the sound of snapping branches subsided, Betony's running footsteps grew more audible with each passing moment, a *pat pat pat* drawing closer. She'd be on us again soon. I was running out of time before Conall turned into a pale victim of Betony's wild gray tantrum.

From a distance came a laugh, a combination of a giggle, a cackle, and a demonic growl. The sound made me shudder, and my hope dwindled to almost nothing as Conall let out an agonized moan and curled around his injury.

I flashed back to days before, when my high priestess had asked me to blend her a salve for her knee. The way I'd known just how to combine the herbs to pull the healing power from the plants. And how many times had I known which herbs to recommend to heal a customer just by touching their hand or arm? If that level of curing power was within my grasp, how much more was possible? And, just as importantly, how fast?

Fuck this shit. Am I the Summate, or am I the Summate?

I closed my eyes and focused. Instead of seeing the obstacle circling us as detrimental, I drew the calamitous whirling sound and strength of the junk tornado into me like fuel. Along with it, I pulled in the light of the glowing orbs surrounding me like the plant using the sun to photosynthesize. I smelled the fear in the sweat of the three of us and extracted strength from that fear energy as well; it stung like an electric shock, but I held on.

Using the Source, I sought power beyond the protective orbs. I tapped into the power of the trees, grass, and flowers growing around us. I drew from the smell of the cemetery and fallen leaves. I sensed the fire in the sun that gave us the moon shining behind the clouds. I felt the strength of the rain in all its many forms—thunderclouds, ocean waves, raging rivers, the rain that fell upon us. All of it was a part of me—of all of us. Earth, air, fire, and water.

Within me, and the love of my friends, I found spirit.

In my mind's eye, I panned the porches of the houses along Oberon Street until I found a large Jack-o'-lantern. Despite her current bent on harming us, I didn't want to kill Betony, but I needed to distract her.

Like the dragon I'd practiced transporting around my shop via telekinesis, I lifted the pumpkin from where it sat on the porch of a Greek-revival style home two doors away. Only instead of moving it from the floor to a shelf, I heaved it like a missile with Betony as its target.

Right in the head, I thought, and I watched as it arched like a round, orange ballistic missile, pegged her mightily, and knocked her off her feet. It would have been humorous if the situation wasn't so goddamn deadly. The wall of junk circling us dropped to the ground almost as quickly as she had. She appeared unconscious, but for how long?

From there, I turned my attention to Conall, who had fallen onto his back. His breathing had gone shallow, and the picket protruded from his middle like the stake from a vampire's heart. I clasped an end and heard Hanna voice her alarm as I yanked the foreign object out.

"It's fine," I said to her, my voice shaky with the energy coursing through me and the fear I was barely keeping at bay. I prayed I was right.

Goddess Hygeia, guide my power. Help me heal him quickly. Super quickly. Like, instantly.

I held my hands out on opposite sides of my body and willed a torrent of healing power into them. My right hand grew icy cold while my left felt as if I held coals growing hotter and hotter, scorching my palms, fingers, and wrist. The energy coursing through me raced like wildly pumping blood, and I felt sweat pour from me, even in the misty rain.

My mind no longer thought in words. The Source became my thoughts, and directed my body like I was a marionette pulled by its strings. I slammed my hands together, and the fiery and freezing sensations blended in a painful bright blue amalgamation that threatened to surge up my arms and set my body on fire. Instead, I crouched and placed my hands on Conall's gushing wound and sent all of that energy into his injury.

He howled in pain, making me wince; I persisted, holding my hands over the deep puncture and willing the severed parts to return to wholeness. Blood seeped onto my fingers, and I grew concerned that my face felt hot until I realized I was crying. Conall writhed under my hands, and I pressed firmly, urging him to be still as the invocation did its work. He let out animal sounds of agony that nearly broke my resolve, but I persisted, chasing him a few inches down the sidewalk when he instinctively slid away from the pain the rapid healing caused.

In a few moments, Conall's breath grew less jagged, and his eyes opened in awe. He moved his body tentatively as he experimented with his rejoined flesh.

"Can you move?" I asked.

His head bobbed, his eyes wide and unsure. "I think so."

I extended a hand. "Come on," I said. "We've got to hustle."

He stood cautiously at first, then more confidently when his body responded as he was used to. A million questions waited behind his eyes, but I could answer them once we were safe.

Our glowing guides pulled tight around us as we moved forward and slowed in a few paces so we could clamber over and through a fallen magnolia tree. I felt my mother's energy pulling me to the right, and I followed its encouragement across the sidewalk and down my walkway, across the veranda, and to the locked door of Witch's Brew. I had rushed out the door in such a hurry that I hadn't grabbed my keys. Crap. We were locked out.

The encroaching sound of flying detritus had resumed, alerting me to Betony's approach. I gripped the door handle and shook it, willing the door to open. I could hardly hear, much less think. I closed my ears to the sound, instead recalling the way my lock felt in my hand when it turned, the way it sounded as it clicked, and the way the bells above the door jingled as the door swung open. The metal pivoted in my palm, and I rushed inside, trailed swiftly by Conall and Hanna. I slammed the door and drew a shuddering breath.

I was safe and warded. I hoped.

Chapter 30

I heard chanting in the distance, and I followed the melody to the back of the house where the coven had joined hands around the clan cauldron. LaDonna broke away from the circle, pulled Luke and Conall's father's hands together, and rushed to my side.

"You look frazzled. Are you OK?" she asked, placing a hand on my arm.

I jumped as a massive crash of thunder was immediately followed by a dazzling lightning flash.

"Betony's back," I told her. Her eyes grew. "Her father—he's possessed her. He found her in the cemetery talking with her grandmother with a board—"

"And she hadn't protected herself first," LaDonna concluded.

I nodded.

"Damn it," she swore. "She should know better. That's just asking for trouble. And tonight, of all nights."

"I know. I told her."

I about flew out of my skin as another deafening clap of thunder boomed, followed by a blinding lightning flash.

"She's striking the house with bolts of lightning," LaDonna said. "She's learning incredibly fast. I think her father is adding to her power with his rage and his reach into the afterlife."

"Fuck," I said, "Do you think the wards will hold?"

LaDonna appeared insulted and motioned to the circle of witches. "With all of us *and* the Summate here?"

It was then that I noticed Jake had joined the circle. "Jake's here?" I whispered, not wanting to distract him from his chant.

"He said he felt 'pulled' to come back," LaDonna replied with a small shrug and a smile. "Is there something about him we should know?"

I thought of Jake's aura radiating from him like solar flares, and I nodded. "He's got a shit-ton of potential if he wants to use it."

LaDonna nodded and gave Jake an appraising look. "Good to know."

Another loud pop, this time the sound of a thick tree branch breaking. Seconds later, an enormous bough swatted against the veranda's wards like a massive wing. I saw Betony's pale, frustrated face between a few limbs as the tree met its match against the warding wall. Her eyes were gray as storm clouds, and her pale face looked drawn and half dead.

"The binding spell isn't working," Hanna said.

"It is," I countered. "The goal was that she wouldn't harm herself or others. She's succeeded, but only once."

"Not for lack of trying."

"True, but we're still standing."

The wind outside picked up, gusting down the chimney flue and stirring the ashes. Through the window, I saw the trees on Oberon Street bending and swaying under the gust. It continued without stopping, like an unending twister, pulling down branches and sending a neighbor's trash can traveling down the road.

Betony crossed the yard to the steps but came no further, hindered by the ward. Nothing had prevented Betony from crossing my threshold before. What stopped her now?

It's not her who's hindered from crossing by the wards. It's her father!

I raced to where the coven was gathered and exclaimed, "We need to bind her dad, not her!" If we can get him out of her, we might get Betony back."

Goddess love the group; they didn't ask any questions, but nodded and awaited direction.

LaDonna hesitated. "We don't have anything of his to add to the spell."

I bit my lip and paused. Had Betony left anything from her home behind that could be used? I had her ankle socks and a few pages of homework I hadn't thrown away. *No, wait!*

"Jake! Your keys! We need your keys!"

Jake blinked as if woken from a trance, taking in my presence as if he hadn't expected to see me.

"Your keys. Do they still have Betony's father's blood on them?"

"God, I hope not," he said, digging them out.

"I hope they do," I replied.

He tried to hand me the keys, but I didn't take them. "Do you know Betony's father's name?"

"Everett," Jake said.

"Same last name? Yarborough?"

He nodded. "Pretty sure. She said her mom had her so her dad wouldn't leave her, so that would make sense."

I turned to LaDonna. "Where's the cord y'all used for the binding spell?"

LaDonna handed me a spool of black twine from the table behind her with a pair of scissors. I measured out about eighteen inches of it, and with Jake's help, I tied it to the keys.

"Will I get these back?" he asked worriedly, and I nodded.

As I spun the twine around the keys, I muttered, "Everett Yarborough, you are bound, from stepping foot again on ground. Your soul I cast from Betony, and as I will, so mote it be."

I grasped Jake's hand and placed the keys inside. "You have to add these to the spell willingly," I told him. His eyes grew, but he nodded.

"For Betony," he said.

We joined the coven at the cauldron, and I took Jake's hand, which held the keys, in mine and raised them high. "Everett Yarborough, you are bound, from stepping foot again on ground. Your soul we cast from Betony, and as we will, so mote it be."

The coven and Jake picked up the call, and our voices became one. Thirteen times, we said the chant, and I sent my thoughts toward Betony. Betony and her many hair colors. Betony and her unceasing curiosity about the craft. Betony, the little mother of her friend group, who she loved so passionately.

Betony who, as we stood against her dark fate, agonized between being proud of her new power, knowing her dad would finally think she was exceptional, and at the same time hating him for being an abusive killer.

It was then it hit me: the sour jar hadn't been for Amber at all. It had been against him.

After the final recitation, I tapped Jake's hand with two fingers to let him know it was time to release the keys. He dropped the keys to his precious Eclipse into the vast depths of the smoking cauldron. The fire jumped, and the incense-laden fumes grew thick with the smell of hot metal, burning twine, and blood transfiguring into the supernatural ropes that sought out and found the spirit of Everett Yarborough.

The sound of rushing wind faded and died, and in the silence that followed it came the sound of falling rain.

An unearthly anguished cry came from just past the veranda, a sound that had no business being as loud as it was, coming from what should have been a human throat.

"Betony," I whispered.

Jake and I broke from the circle, dashed out the door and past the veranda, where Betony stood hunched over, her hands on the steps.

She's past the ward. Her father is gone.

"Betony?"

"Don't talk to me," she said, her voice raspy.

"Bet, I'm here," Jake said, and she looked up, surprised. "Are you OK? Can I help you up?"

She pursed her lips and eyed me with mild suspicion. She was still upset, and perhaps justifiably so, but her father's rage had disappeared.

"Sure," she said.

She tried to stand and staggered. Jake rushed down the steps and slung a hand across her back, propping her up so she could scale the stairs.

"Come on," he said, "You've got this."

As he aided her into the shop, I headed upstairs out of earshot and pressed the buttons on my phone to reach one of my most-used contacts. After a few rings, the familiar sound of officer Kenny Hendricks's voice came through the phone.

"Kenny, I need your help."

"Oh, lord. It's almost midnight, Murphy. I ain't got time for this. What'd you do now?" His tone was light and teasing despite sounding tired as well.

Where to start? What does he need to know?

I reached for the Source to guide me and realized that although I had released it, the Source had never let me go. The power had always been there, inside me, waiting for me to recognize its presence. I hadn't been letting it in so much as opening myself up to the power I'd had coursing within me all along.

I closed my gaping mouth and swallowed past an enormous lump that had formed in my throat.

I am the Summate. It weighed heavy on my spirit and yet felt... right.

My reports to Officer Hendricks often started with a sigh and a resigned feeling of despondence. Life as a gray was all I'd known and all I'd expected, and it had sucked. I'd shut myself away from everyone. Life wasn't living so much as survival and protecting others from the damage I inflicted.

With Betony as the gray, perhaps this story could have a new ending. With the coven and a Summate learning alongside her, maybe we could help her learn how to control her power while I learned to free mine more. It might be a long shot, but I had hope. Like LaDonna said, without a bit of chaos, the universe would die of entropy. *Maybe I can balance her if she lets me. My power will be greater, once I stop being so afraid of it.*

"Murphy?"

"I'm here, Kenny."

I began the story.

Epilogue

Colorful Yuletide décor festooned the entry of the Leland County Youth Detention Center, splashes of cheer in stark contrast to the institutional beige and gray painted cinderblock walls. A short, scrawny Christmas tree stood in the corner, and underneath it scattered presents boasted oversized tags with uber-southern names like Jim-Bob and Betty-Sue.

"You're sure she wants to see me?" I asked for the dozenth time, and Jake's and Lorina's heads both bobbed in joint confirmation. Their affirmation aside, I remembered the suspicious look she'd given me the last time I'd seen her and a reluctance made my steps heavy.

Betony's privileges had been very restricted: no visitors, no letters, no emails, no phone calls. This trip to the detention center was strictly a favor of the courts and only because she'd been doing exemplarily well.

The court had determined that Betony wouldn't be returning to her mother once she was released. An investigation was ongoing to see if it could be proven that she and Betony's father had committed the coven murders sixteen years ago, but I wasn't holding out hope for a conviction. Her mother did, however, admit to turning a blind eye to her husband's abuse; at the very least, she'd do some time for that. I did, however, have some positive news I wanted to share with her, if she was inclined to accept it.

"She specifically told me to bring you," Lorina said, taking the pen from the clipboard at the bulletproof reception window and adding her name to the visitor list before passing the pen to Jake. She was left-handed, I noted. So was Jake. Why did I always forget that? "She got special privileges to see people in person for the holiday, and the one person she wanted to see more than anyone is you."

I added my name below Jake's and followed them across the room. We took seats in the institutional metal and plastic chairs lining the walls and waited for about twenty minutes before a guard called us back to the space where the Betony was being allowed to see visitors. He unlocked a heavy metal gray door and waved us inside.

I was ready to retreat if she showed any sign that I wasn't welcome. I may be the Summate, but I didn't want to battle if I didn't need to, especially in public where someone might get hurt. Instead, I touched a larger portion of Source power and sought the energy waves for Betony's frequency—a new talent I'd developed. I wasn't sure I'd recognize it, but once I felt its presence, there was no denying it. Gray energy has a unique vibration, like touching an electrical tingle under a silk scarf.

Betony waited for us with a relaxed smile on her face. She'd lost some of her curviness, and about two inches of brown roots topped her long hair, which had faded from bright raspberry to baby pink.

"Come on, Murphy." Lorina reached around Jake and grasped my arm in her surprisingly strong, twiggy hand. She yanked me forward and pulled me toward Betony's table like I was a kindergartner with separation anxiety on her first day of school.

When I met Betony's eyes, the signs of malice or resentment were gone. Instead, she was the same sharp-eyed, sweet, baby-faced teen who'd visited my coffee shop for the past three years. Her eyes were hazel again, but this time with a beautiful gray ring around the pupils.

"It's OK, Mama Murph," she said. "I'm OK."

Her soothing voice touched my heart. My hand went to my chest, and a relieved smile spread across my face as I fought the urge to cry. I sat across from her at the table and reached forward to clasp her hand but drew back. It was Betony.

To my amazement, she reached forward and gripped my hand in hers. As our hands touched, I allowed a hint more of Source energy to flow. Gone was the erratic, sickly aura she'd once displayed. In its place, a silvery-gray aura stretched to a healthy perimeter around her. She fairly glowed. It was beautiful.

She smiled her familiar smile, and I felt an odd click of energy flow between us. Her gray aura touched my indigo, and our silvers meshed at the edges like old friends.

"You've been practicing," I said admiringly.

She shrugged, withdrew her hand, and broke the connection. "I've always wanted to learn shadow work, and it's easy to do with all these broken people around here to help."

"Good for you," I said, and meant it. If she'd been performing shadow work with any success, she'd done volumes of introspection in the time she'd been detained.

"It helps a lot to have a place to use my strength," she said. "Keeps the lightbulbs from popping out and the showers from going cold." She laughed, and her humor at having to focus her gray power down a particular channel sounded so healthy I knew she'd handle the chaos far better than I ever had.

This is why Betony was the perfect gray witch. Her love of people and her need to help them deal with their shadow selves and the chaos in their lives were integral to who she was; she'd found it impossible to separate the two. I loved intensely, but narrowly, and my circle of friends was modest. Unlike her, I'd found comfort in my isolation. Maybe Betony could help me with that.

"How many days now?" Lorina asked, draping her lanky body across the table and leaning on her arms.

"Fifty-six," Betony answered, her jaw propped up on a perched hand. "Not that I'm counting."

"Any idea where you'll be going after this?" Jake asked. From the sound of his question, it wasn't the first time he'd inquired. I wondered when he'd had a chance to speak to her before. Court, perhaps.

Betony shook her head, and her eyes dropped to the laminated tabletop. She ran a thin fingernail through a set of initials carved there. "I might be a ward of the state," she mumbled. "I've got to go someplace until I'm nineteen. Freaking Alabama and its ridiculous age of majority."

"Um… I have a solution for you," I said. "If you want it."

Shock registered on her face, and she blinked as she met my gaze. "You do?" The hope in her voice made my heart ache for her.

"I know a woman who is excellent at helping someone with chaos energy," I said, "and she's been talking to the court about being your guardian."

"Who? You?"

I shook my head. "LaDonna. She said she'd be more than happy to take you in and start teaching you the way she taught me after my mother died."

Betony jumped up from her seat and jumped up and down in excitement. "LaDonna? The high priestess? Really?"

Her pure joy was contagious, and I smiled so broadly my face hurt. This was the Betony I knew.

"We'd have to clear it with the state. Given her history with me, there's a good chance it will go through without a hitch, though."

"Murphy—" Words wouldn't come. Instead, she dove at me and embraced me in a fierce hug. "Thank you, Murphy. Thank you, thank you."

"Merry Christmas, Betony," I said.

"Blessed Yule," she added. "And blessed be."

"Blessed be," Jake and I agreed.

Here is an excerpt from *Blood Tribe*, coming March 2022.

Book One of Iris Kain's *Blood Tribe* trilogy!

October 1943

Vivian's only clue that her mother was home was the presence of their run-down Ford in the driveway. The house was silent and tidy as usual. She walked through the entry, hung her jacket on the brass coatrack, and straight into the roomy living room to the focal point—the radio. It stood as high as Vivian's waist, and even though on cloudy days the reception was at best so-so, it was her mother's pride and joy. She turned the power knob. Duke Ellington's "Mood Indigo" poured from the speakers.

She walked over to the oak rolltop desk and sat down in the high-backed chair. She tried to dispel the unforgettable sensation of Jude's touch, but the more she tried to distract herself, the more pressing the memory became.

Duke Ellington ended, and Tommy Dorsey picked up with "Marie" on his famous trombone.

Maybe if I try to write Phillip a letter, she decided. She rolled back the cover and reached into the right-hand drawer where her mother kept the paper. She grabbed a pen, dipped the nib into the ink, and determined she would write whatever came to mind.

"My Dearest Phillip," she wrote, and was stumped. She sat back and tried to think through the past few days to find a topic to write about, but all that came to mind was Jude's silk voice, his touch, the graceful way he danced, and the soulful voice of the crooning singer.

Her hand started for the page two or three times as she considered telling him about the dance, but she stopped herself. *And what would you write?* "Well, the American Legion Hall held a dance, but I only stayed for a few minutes. Ruth kicked me out after I started flirting with someone." *Don't be stupid.*

The phone rang. Vivian leaped from her chair and nearly spilled the ink. It was late; her mother would most likely be asleep. She reached for the phone.

"Hello?"

"Vivian?" Wesley's voice barely carried over the background noise.

He had called from the hall. "Is that you?"

"Yes, Wesley," she responded. "What's up?"

"Well, I'm not sure," Wesley said. "Did Ruth say anything to you about when she was planning on going home?"

"Um, no," Vivian tried to recall any part of her conversation with Ruth she might have forgotten. Nothing came to mind.

"I don't see her," he said. "I was wondering if she'd said anything to you."

"Sorry, but I don't think I can help you. I don't know anything that you don't."

"Well, if she calls you, let me know. I'm going to go see if maybe I missed her," Wesley said. His voice didn't sound hopeful.

"Keep me posted, all right?" Vivian asked.

"I'll let you know as soon as I find her," Wesley said. They hung up.

Her concern rose. It was unlike Ruth to wander off by herself. Over-protective parents, loving friends, and a doting boyfriend—now fiancé—had made it an uncommon instance for Ruth to be alone. That Wesley had to look for her was puzzling and a little disturbing. *Well, it was a busy night,* she reasoned and tried to put it out of her head.

She sat down with pen and paper again and forced herself to pen a page full of nonsense and small talk. Agitated, she put up her writing utensils, closed the desk, and went to bed.

That night, she tried to steer her dreams toward rational thoughts of Phillip and marriage and their future together, but it didn't work. She was haunted by nightmares of a beautiful, dark man who seduced her, no matter how hard she tried to ward him off.

⋐ ⋑

Her mother's voice woke her in the morning.

"Vivian, honey, you have a phone call."

She sat up sluggishly and peered through half-open eyes at her bed-side clock. It was only a few minutes after six in the morning. Anyone who knew her well enough to call her should know that she wouldn't be crawling out of bed for another hour. She wondered who it was as she slouched into her robe, found her slippers with blurry eyes, and stumbled to the living room.

Her mother waited in the doorway to ensure Vivian was awake. As usual, Rose Black had pulled herself together early, a store-bought cotton dress pulled snugly over her trim figure, a cup of coffee in her hand, lipstick blotted on the bone rose cup. When Vivian managed to make it to the living room, Rose smiled and handed her the telephone.

"Hello?" She fought to keep the grogginess from her voice but failed.

"Vivian? It's Wesley," he stuttered. He sounded as though he were trying to talk around a bone stuck in his throat. "Listen, I need to talk to you as soon as possible. It's urgent. I'd have come over to tell you, but they needed me here...."

"Wesley, you're not making sense. We're talking now. Why would you come over? What's wrong?"

"I don't want to tell you over the phone—"

"Wesley, what happened? Is this about Ruth? Don't make me worry. Tell me what happened."

There was a sigh and a choked sob. Wesley was *crying*!

Oh, this is bad.

Vivian waited with a furrowed brow for Wesley to find his voice. All thoughts of sleep vanished. She tapped a nervous foot on the floor. Her mother brought her a steaming cup of coffee, and Vivian nodded a thank you rather than speak. She didn't want to interrupt Wesley. Rose disappeared, probably to the kitchen, to finish reading the morning paper.

"It's about Ruth, Vivian. Remember how I couldn't find her at the dance?"

"Yes, of course, I remember."

"Well, I never did find her. I asked some people if they had seen her, but they hadn't." He drew in a shuddering breath and continued. "A bunch of us started looking for her, calling around, that sort of thing. I knew if she had left, she would have gone with us. I knew something was wrong...." He broke off and sobbed hysterically.

Vivian was now desperate to know what had happened, but part of her knew. Somehow, she knew.

"Wesley, what happened?" she barked. There was another pause, and Vivian tapped her foot even harder. She wanted to stretch her arm through the phone and force him to talk. The wait was torture.

"I'm going to come over," he sniffled. "I don't want to say this over—"

"Wesley William Scott, you tell me right this second! Where the hell is Ruth? What happened?"

He still did not want to say. This time, Vivian swore she could have reached through the phone and grabbed him by his shirtfront and shook him until he spoke, but she had to wait. She endured another static-filled, shaky breath but didn't interrupt.

"I took the woods behind the hall. I don't know why I looked there, but I did. She shouldn't have been there. Now I wish... Why couldn't someone else have...?"

"Have *what*, Wesley?"

His voice struggled, delivering the news in fits and starts. "I found her, Viv. I found her. Dead. I. Found. Her. Dead. *Dead*. She's gone, Viv."

"*No*," Vivian murmured. "How?"

"How?" Wesley sounded angry. "I don't know. All they tell me is that she lost her blood somehow."

"Lost it? How does a person *lose* their blood?"

"From the looks of it, she lost a lot on the ground."

"Wesley!" Vivian cried.

"I'm sorry," he apologized. "I'm so... so.... Listen, is it all right if I come over? I'd like to talk to you. I need to talk to someone."

"Of course," she said. She understood. She could use someone to talk to as well. She wasn't sobbing yet, but her throat felt obstructed, and tears poured down her cheeks.

"I'll be there soon," he said

"All right."

She hung up the phone in a stupor.

Ruth... gone? How? She didn't understand. How does someone lose their blood and die? She'd never heard of such a thing. It sounded like some crazy jungle disease or something out of a novel, not something that happened in New Bridgeport, Michigan. She stood on shaky legs and walked to her room, her coffee forgotten.

Hot tears poured down her cheeks as she lay down on her bed. Ruth, her closest friend, was gone. While her mind grasped hold of the concept, her heart still refused to budge. She saw, in her mind, Ruth's flustered face as she forced her to leave the hall the night before. She saw her rosy cheeks, her dark, curly hair, the rare determined set of her mouth. What had possessed her to go into the woods that late at night? She knew Ruth–she wasn't a nature-lover, no matter what time of day it was. The thought of woods crawling with heaven knew what kinds of bugs and four-legged creatures wouldn't be attractive to her.

Poor Wesley. What is he going to do? Ruth was his whole life. How will he go on without her?

As she sobbed into her pillow, she wondered how she would get along as well.

CR ɾɾ

By the time Wesley arrived, Vivian had showered and put on a fresh pot of coffee. She nearly forgot to comb her hair, and when she looked at her reflection in the mirror, her eyes red-ringed and swollen, she looked as if she hadn't had any sleep at all. Her mother had asked what was wrong, and after finding out a few details, graciously stepped back to let her daughter deal with the situation the way she usually did. On her own

Wesley looked even worse than she did. His button-down shirt and slacks were as wrinkled as if he had slept in them. When she stopped to think about it, she recognized the shirt and slacks as the same ones he had been wearing when he dropped her off last night. His eyes had circles so dark it looked as if someone had slugged him. His sandy hair was uncharacteristically unkempt, and his face was a sickening gray-white under his tan.

She let him into the house and showed him the way to the large, white kitchen. She handed him a cup of black coffee, and Wesley looked at the fabric-covered white chairs nervously, afraid to sit down in his dirty slacks.

"It's all right," Vivian assured him, sitting across from the chair she directed him to take. "They're washable."

He sat down and sipped his coffee, his face covered with a distracted expression. His eyes steered clear of hers as if he feared she blamed him somehow for Ruth's death.

"I don't know where to begin," he murmured. "It all started so quickly. I couldn't find her. I asked around, tried to find folks who might've known where she was. No one knew anything. So I called you, then I checked again, but that was no good. She just wasn't there. That's when I started to panic.

"I got the guys together, and we started to call people, friends she might have left with for one reason or another. Nobody knew anything, and by now, it was getting late—around midnight or so, I figure. So the guys and I all wandered around looked for her. Thought maybe she'd walked home, and we just missed her. But I drove the route to her house and didn't see her, and her folks said she wasn't there. And then *they're* worried. That's when someone called the police—her father, I imagine.

"The guys suggested we start to search the whole area for her, on foot, you know? I thought it was a great idea. I knew that Ruth wouldn't.... Well, you know Ruth. She never does the unpredictable. That's why I was so upset.

"The other fellas, they took different roads. Thought maybe she just took a long way home or something. I took the woods behind the hall with Artie and Frank and one or two others."

He paused to drink a sip of coffee. Vivian followed suit. Her throat had grown dry as she listened to the details of the hours preceding her friend's death. He put the chintz cup back in its saucer, and it struck Vivian how strong and capable his hands looked holding the tiny piece of china. He didn't look as though he felt capable at that moment, though. He looked beaten. Defeated.

He continued.

"I don't know why I took the woods. It was the last place I suspected she'd be. I think maybe somehow, I knew... It only took a couple of minutes for me to find her. Even in the pitch-dark part of the woods, she was so pale...."

Vivian didn't press for details. She didn't want them. He had already hinted at how gruesome the scene was, and she didn't want to picture it; it would make it too easy to imagine how her friend may have suffered. Yet he looked so burdened by pain and confusion Vivian didn't ask him to stop. He hadn't stopped staring at the tile floor since he took his first sip of coffee, and his voice was level and detached. He needed to unburden himself by sharing the details with someone. She sat, her arms on the table, her eyes unblinking and dry, and listened to the bizarre scenario.

"The coroner explained that her body was drained of nearly all its blood. Imagine that. Like a Goddamn vampire got a hold of it. Oh, sorry. You know I don't like to swear in front of a lady, but jeez. It looked to me like there was plenty of blood there. It was all over the place."

He broke off for a moment to regain his composure, his eyes brimming with tears. Vivian waited for him to go on.

"I'm really sorry to be the one who has to tell you this. I didn't know where else to go to. You were Ruth's best friend. I suppose a part of me thought you'd want to know."

"I did, in a way," she admitted. *Although I could have done without all the details.* "I don't understand it any better than you do, but it helps me to know I can be here for you."

"You don't know why Ruth was in the woods, do you?"

Vivian shook her head and agreed it was both puzzling and maddening.

They finished their coffee in silence. Vivian struggled for something to say, but nothing came to mind. They were both lost in thoughts of Ruth—memories of her life, marveling at her sudden death. Wesley patted her hand several times in reassurance, and she did the same as if by strengthening each other, they could help themselves.

The phone rang. Vivian crossed the kitchen, entered the living room, and answered it. She guessed it would be another grieving friend—Daisy Milner from English class, possibly. She had been a close friend to Vivian and Ruth. But no one was there.

She hung up.

She returned to the kitchen, where she found Wesley on his feet. The two of them made plans to visit Ruth's family in an hour or two after Vivian had freshened up. The phone rang again.

Vivian held up a finger, and Wesley nodded. She entered the living room yet again and answered the phone.

Once more, no one was there.

"That's odd," she commented. She looked up, and Wesley was watching her. She flushed, embarrassed that he caught her talking to herself, but he didn't seem to mind.

"I'll be around in a little while to drive you to the family's house if you'd like," he offered.

"Thank you. That would be nice," she said, and the phone rang a third time. An annoyed expression crossed her face, but she lifted the receiver.

"Hello?"

"Vivian?" It was the voice of her neighbor, Frances Drake, New Bridgeport's leading rumormonger. Vivian had a vague memory of seeing Frances at the dance the night before, on the arm of her very long-standing, very henpecked boyfriend, Paul. Frances had waved briefly before catching Rita Schmidt by the shoulder and giving her an intense conspiratorial look, and running her mouth at what appeared to be faster than the speed of thought. Which, knowing Frances, might not be too far from the truth. Still, Vivian mused, she was mostly harmless, as long as she listened more than she shared.

"Yes, Frances."

"Have you heard about Ruth? Of *course* you have. What was I *thinking*? It's *awful*. And to think, it might have been any one of us."

"Any one of us?"

Wesley motioned at his watch and mouthed the words, "Two hours." Vivian nodded and waved as he let himself out.

"You know Ruthie would never go into the woods alone at night. She's not *that* ridiculous. And from what I heard, her body was in an awful state."

Vivian ignored the comment that her friend was ridiculous and said only, "Yes, Wesley told me."

"Wesley? Oh, yes. Poor Wesley. So, he's been with you, *hmm*? Well, at least he has a *friend* to talk to." Her voice held a knowing tone that made Vivian bristle, and her mouth opened to rebut the implications, but Frances continued too quickly. "Well, my *father's* friend works at the coroner's office, and he won't stop talking about it. Honestly, Vivian, it's *terrible* the way they're making such a *dreadful* commotion over this."

I'm sure you're terribly *upset,* Vivian thought. Frances continued seemingly without taking a breath. "I know it's not often someone passes in that fashion around here—you know, murdered—but they woke me up at five this morning, and the phone hasn't stopped ringing since."

Vivian didn't doubt that Frances had been on the telephone all morning, but she would have wagered that Frances was the one doing the ringing. She backed out of the conversation as tactfully as possible. Talking about Ruth with Wesley, who had loved her every bit as much—possibly more—than Vivian did was one thing. On the other hand, talking to Frances was like trying to tiptoe through her mother's flowerbeds blindfolded—she never knew when she was going to step somewhere she shouldn't.

She headed down the hall to her room, opened her closet door, and scanned the rack for her navy dress—she didn't own anything black—when the phone rang again. She hesitated and let it ring twice before deciding to answer it. It didn't seem fair to put her mother out—it was most likely for her, anyway.

This is the last call. I'll wait outside, so I don't have to hear the phone if I must, she thought as she lifted the receiver.

The line was dead.

Made in the USA
Columbia, SC
03 November 2022

70385842R00112